SUBSTANTIAL RISK

David Brunelle Legal Thriller #5

STEPHEN PENNER

ISBN-13: 978-0692255537
ISBN-10: 0692255532

Substantial Risk

This is a work of fiction. Any similarity with real persons or events is purely coincidental. Persons, events, and locations are either the product of the author's imagination, or used fictitiously.

Joy Lorton, Editor.
Cover by Nathan Wampler Book Covers.

SUBSTANTIAL
RISK

A person is reckless if he or she knows of and disregards a substantial risk that a wrongful act may occur and this disregard is a gross deviation from conduct that a reasonable person would exercise in the same situation.

State of Washington
Pattern Criminal Jury Instruction 10.03

CHAPTER 1

The Cu-CUM-ber Club.

The sign flashed a lurid purple and green, as if arguing with the red and blue strobe of the police cars parked in front of the 'business.' The middle syllable flashed the brightest.

David Brunelle, homicide prosecutor with the King County Prosecutor's Office, squeezed his car into a 'loading only' spot across the street and stepped out into the frenzy. Seattle's Capitol Hill neighborhood was euphemistically described as 'eclectic.' In fact, it was ground zero for both the city's arts community and its gay community. There were arts and gays elsewhere of course, but if you wanted to see a 6'4" drag queen walking down the street playing the accordion, then you went to Capitol Hill. And when the cops showed up, the locals spilled out of their lofts and studios to make sure their safe place was still safe. It was. Except for one poor soul inside the Cu-CUM-ber Club.

"Hey, Dave," Seattle P.D. Detective Larry Chen greeted Brunelle as the D.A. crossed the street and ducked under the crime scene tape. "Welcome to the show."

Brunelle nodded toward the sign. "You should have said, 'Welcome to the club.'"

Chen grinned. "Sorry, Dave. I don't belong to this particular club, so I can't welcome you to it. But trust me, there's a show inside. Or there was. But it went horribly wrong."

Brunelle frowned thoughtfully as he examined the exterior of the club. There really wasn't any doubt it was a sex club. No need to hide that up here. The gift shop Brunelle had parked in front of had greeting cards in its front window featuring artistic photos of pierced genitals. Capitol Hill wasn't ashamed of itself. It wasn't shy either.

This particular sex club seemed to feature some sort of fetish culture. There was a definite dungeon theme going on with the exterior decorating. Brunelle found himself curious about what was inside. That gift shop had a lot of Curious George dolls in its window too.

"Something went wrong, huh?" Brunelle finally replied, pulling his mind back to why he was there. The 1 a.m. phone call about the new homicide on 15th Avenue. "So is the body still inside?"

Chen nodded. "Yep." He looked at the dungeon doors, then back to Brunelle. "Ready to go in?"

Brunelle looked at the doors too, their faux stone paint job daring him inside. He smiled despite the circumstances. "Yep."

* * *

Brunelle anticipated experiencing several different feelings in addition to his curiosity, but the overwhelming emotion he felt as they stepped inside was disappointment. He'd expected dark and seedy, with dim lights and scantily clad customers. Devices and noises, music and dancers, lions and tigers and bears. He wasn't exactly sure. But he was expecting a sex club. What he found, of course, was a crime scene.

All the lights were up. There were no customers, just cops. Fully dressed and definitely not dancing. There were also what appeared to be a couple of employees—civilians who wouldn't normally be allowed inside otherwise. One such civilian hurried up to them, obviously upset. He was tall, with receding brown hair and a small belly fighting against his white button-up shirt. He wore glasses that were a bit too large and thick enough to distort his eyes.

"Detective Chen!" he called out. Obviously Chen had been inside already. Of course he had, Brunelle realized. That's how Chen knew to call him. "Detective Chen, I just wanted to tell you, Michael is in my office."

Chen nodded to the man. "Thank you, Mr. Gillespie."

"Who's Michael?" Brunelle asked as Mr. Gillespie scurried away to attend to whatever the manager of a sex club needs to attend to when there's been a murder in the club.

"Michael's our killer," Chen replied.

Brunelle raised an eyebrow. "He stuck around?"

Chen nodded. "The victim was his long-time girlfriend."

Brunelle wasn't that surprised. Domestic violence homicides were unfortunately common. Although not so much in public. "What happened?"

Chen opened his mouth to explain, then closed it again. "Come on, Dave. You should see it for yourself."

* * *

They walked down a long narrow hallway with exposed concrete floors and framed photos on the walls. The photos, Brunelle didn't even pretend not to notice, were of various clients performing various acts with various other clients and equipment. Most of the identities seemed to be hidden beneath masks and/or said equipment. He finally tore his eyes away when they reached the private room that housed the remains of the victim.

"In here." Chen gestured into the room. Brunelle hesitated, then walked in first, uncertain what he'd find.

Like the main room, the lights were all on, thereby

destroying the mood that likely existed during regular operating protocols. Also doing violence to the mood were the two police officers in full uniform photographing the scene—although Brunelle could imagine circumstances where that might work into the fantasy. The final nail in the eroticism coffin was the dead body on the dais in the center of the room.

The only thing helping the mood at all was the woman attending to the body: Brunelle's girlfriend, medical examiner Kat Anderson. When Chen had called Brunelle, he'd jokingly asked if Kat was lying next to him. But they hadn't moved in together—not yet, anyway—and it was a school night. Kat had a teenage daughter and, girlfriend or not, she was a mom first.

Brunelle stepped over to where Kat was visually examining the bindings on the body, her hand hovering over, but not quite touching them. She was lost in thought and hadn't reacted to their arrival.

He knelt down next to her. "Dr. Anderson, I presume?"

She snapped her gaze at him and smiled. "David. Fancy meeting you here."

Brunelle looked around. "We should try this place under different circumstances."

Kat grinned. "You think so, huh?" She nodded back toward the hallway. "Have you seen the cock-and-ball cages yet?"

Brunelle's eyebrows shot up. He hadn't seen those. He didn't even know what they were. But the name suggested he'd rather not find out. A blush burned his cheeks and he changed the subject. "So what happened here?"

What had happened there was open for all to see—at least the part up until the victim had died. She was a woman—that much was obvious. Her breasts were completely exposed and she wasn't wearing any clothes below her waist, except for a pair of knee-high, high heel boots. Her ankles were tied to the back of her thighs with expertly knotted rope and her face was covered in some sort of leather hood. The only openings were for her eyes and her mouth, but the one for her mouth seemed superfluous since the mouth was gagged with a red rubber ball tied around the back of her head with black straps. There was also a decoratively applied coil of rope around her throat, raising from her collarbone to her jaw, then secured behind her to the rope on her ankles.

It was a lot to take in all at once. Brunelle pointed to the woman's arms, which were held behind her back and straight down by a long leather sheath that laced up the back. "And what the hell is that?"

"It's called an arm-sleeve," Kat replied. She shook her head. "You really should get out more, David."

The blush deepened. "So what did she die of?" he deflected, "Embarrassment?"

Kat shook her head. "Oh, very sensitive. Wow. Maybe don't say that in front of the jury."

Brunelle regretted the joke. It was disrespectful. Maybe more importantly, it was unprofessional. So he got professional again. "I only get in front of a jury if this is homicide." He nodded toward the bound corpse in front of them. "How did she die?"

Kat looked again at the young woman's remains. She frowned thoughtfully. "I'm guessing she was strangled to death, by the rope around her throat."

Brunelle looked at the ligature. "Good guess."

Kat shrugged. "Maybe. I'll need to do a full autopsy. My suspicion is that the rope alone probably wasn't enough, but add the leather over her nose and the ball in her mouth, and I'm guessing she asphyxiated."

Brunelle looked again at the dead woman. If they'd found a body bound like that in the trunk of a car or somebody's basement, there would have been no doubt it was murder. Somehow, though, at that club, the bindings themselves seemed to suggest accident.

He stood up again. "Come on, Larry," he said to Chen. "Let's go talk to Master Michael."

CHAPTER 2

Master Michael was sitting in the office of the previously encountered club manager. Patrick Gillespie was in there with him, trying to make distracting small talk, while a patrol officer silently guarded the door. All three of them were awaiting the return of the detective. Brunelle peered inside to get a look at their suspected killer. Michael was probably late 30s, with thick black hair, no shirt, and black leather pants; he'd pulled on a light jacket to cover his bare chest, which was muscular enough, but nothing special.

Brunelle was satisfied with his glimpse and stepped to the side of the doorframe, still in the hallway. He could hear from there. He didn't need to be in the room. In fact, he didn't want to be in the room. If Master Michael confessed, Brunelle would be calling Chen as a witness to the confession. He didn't need to muddy the waters by being in the room at the time. Still, he wanted to hear what Michael had to say, so he nodded at Chen then jerked his thumb toward the office. Chen showed his understanding with his own nod then stepped inside alone.

"Hello, Michael," Chen began. "I'm Larry Chen. I'm a detective with Seattle P.D. I need to talk with you about Tina's death."

"Okay," Michael croaked. "I—" but his thought trailed off.

Brunelle was listening but let his eyes wander across the hallway to more of the photographs he had noticed earlier.

"Let's start with the basics," Chen said. Brunelle heard a chair scrape across the floor and the sound of the detective dropping his heavy frame into it. "What's your full name?"

"Michael Edward Atkins."

"And what was Tina's full name?"

A pause, then, "Christina Lynn Belfair." There was a crack in Michael's voice as he said her first name. Brunelle frowned. He didn't need that kind of remorse showing to the jury. On the other hand, it bode well for the likelihood of an impending confession.

"What was your relationship with Tina?" Chen asked.

Another hesitation. Finally, "She was my girlfriend."

"Girlfriend?" Chen repeated back. "Nothing more? Not fiancée or anything?"

"Well," Michael answered, "it's kind of complicated. We've been together for almost five years. But we didn't have any definite plans to get married. But we were exclusive. She was my sub and I was her dom."

Brunelle raised an eyebrow. *Oh, this should be good.*

"Could you explain that a little more?" Chen asked. "I get this is some kind of sex club, but I might need you to spell it out for me. Sorry."

Michael exhaled audibly. "Right, Sure. No worries. It's just. Well, that's why we came here. There are a lot of people who don't get it. It's kind of tiring trying to explain it. And I'm not going to try to convince you it's okay. It's okay. And if you can't handle that, then, well, you can fuck off."

Nice. Brunelle smiled. *Maybe this guy won't be so great on the stand after all.*

"You might want to rein it in a bit," Chen replied, an edge to his voice. "I'm just trying to figure out what happened. Nobody's judging you."

Not for the freak sex stuff, Brunelle thought. *The whole killing your girlfriend thing might be different.* He glanced from a photo of someone 'dressed' amazingly like a pony—down to the blinders—to another of a woman whose proclivity for leather seemed to reach everywhere but her sexual body parts, which were, of course, completely exposed. The mask reminded him of the one the victim was wearing, except that it allowed for a long ponytail out the back.

"Okay, okay, sorry," Michael replied. "It's just. I'm sorry. This is a lot. I just... I loved her. And now she's gone and..."

Michael stopped and Brunelle could hear him choking back his tears. "I just loved her," Michael said. "That's all."

Several seconds of silence followed. Chen must have decided that was in fact all, or at least it was enough for right then. He moved on. "Tell me what happened."

There was another pause as Michael sniffed back the tears and refocused himself on answering the questions. Facts were always easier to talk about than feelings. Leather-clad 'master' or not, he was still a man.

"Uh, okay," he started. "We came here tonight for a session. Nothing special. We like to come here a few times a month. We have our own dungeon at home—"

Of course you do, Brunelle thought with a roll of his eyes. Still, he was enjoying the photos on the walls a bit more than he might have admitted. *Was that a stockade?*

"—but it can be fun to be out too. Part of enjoying each other is letting others know we enjoy each other."

"Okay," Chen said. It was noncommittal, but encouraged more talking.

"So, anyway. Tina likes—liked," Michael corrected darkly, "the pain side of it, but I enjoy the restraint a little more. She's more

S&M and I'm more B&D, but we made it work. Taking turns, just like who's going to do the dishes, ya know?"

Wow. This guy is totally nuts, Brunelle thought, but his attention was divided by a photograph of an attractive brunette standing at attention, her wrists and ankles apparently cuffed. *And she is totally hot.*

"So what was tonight?" Chen asked, as if they were discussing whose turn it was to drive to church.

"Tonight was restraint," Michael explained. "She knew I'd give her some pain too. Some lashes on her ass, but only after I had her fully restrained. So it was me deciding to give her what she needed. So there was no doubt I was in control."

Brunelle snapped his full attention back to the interview. He needed to listen. Then he noticed one more photograph...

"So did you guys have sex then?" Chen asked, a bit brusquely.

"What?" Michael replied, a bit surprised. "Oh, no. We hadn't gotten that far. It can take a while to do all those restraints. That's part of the fun. It's a kind of foreplay. I mean, I was going to enter her, but not right away. It's not about that. Well, not just that. It's about intimacy and trust and love."

"Right," Chen interjected. "So what happened?"

"I'm not sure," Michael admitted. "I mean I'd finished the bindings and she was ready. I was going to play with her for a bit. Give her pleasure. Get her close to cuming, but not let her. Then we'd move on to some other stuff. Clamps, clothespins, toys. But then I noticed she wasn't responding to me. At first I thought she was trying to play with me. To resist by failing to respond, by not giving me the moans I was causing in her. But then she didn't respond to the lashes either. Nothing. Not even the coat hanger. That's when I knew there was a problem. I checked and she wasn't breathing. I tried to undo the bindings, but my hands were shaking so bad I couldn't grasp the rope. So I panicked and ran for help. Jim here came in and I just fell back against the wall. He checked for a pulse, then turned and said we better call the police."

"I'm sorry, Michael," Gillespie said. "I had to call the authorities. There are rules."

"Don't be sorry, Jim," Michael replied. "I know. It's not your fault. It's mine. All mine. Tina's dead, and it's all my fault."

Brunelle heard Chen's chair slide backwards as he stood up. "You're right, Mr. Atkins, it is your fault. You're under arrest for murder."

Brunelle half-expected Michael to protest. Something like, 'Murder? But I loved her!' But there was no protest. No words at all. Brunelle listened as Chen fastened on the handcuffs and Jim Gillespie again said, "I'm sorry, Michael."

Chen led Michael out of the room and down the hallway. Brunelle trailed behind, his work there finished.

"I'll check in with you later," Brunelle yelled after the retreating Chen. Chen acknowledged the call with a raise of his hand. Then Brunelle turned and ducked back into the room where the body was found.

But Kat was gone already.

So was the body, but he didn't really care about that. He just wanted to see his girlfriend. He was finally used to that term. 'Girlfriend.' Wasn't that what Master Michael had called Tina? His girlfriend?

The one remaining forensics officer was taking a few 'after' photographs of the room. He stopped to look up at Brunelle, but Brunelle waved him back to his work. It was time for him to go.

He'd call Kat later and ask her about the autopsy. In the meantime, he could decide whether to tell her what he thought he'd seen in that last photograph: young defense attorney Robyn Dunn's unique one-sided, barely visible beneath her studded leather mask.

CHAPTER 3

After a few hours of sleep, Brunelle got to work early and found himself summoned to the office of his boss, the elected prosecutor Matt Duncan. Duncan was on the phone, but not because he wanted to be. It just wouldn't stop ringing.

"We'll review all the evidence," he was saying, "and make a charging decision based on the facts and the law. Right. Yes. Exactly. Okay, thanks, Ken. I'll know more later this morning. Bye."

Duncan hung up again and shouted out to his secretary, "Hold my calls for a few minutes, Tammy. I need to talk to Dave and figure out what the hell is going on."

"CNN is on hold," Tammy shouted back, "Do you want me to take a message?"

Duncan thought for a moment, then replied. "Yes. It's just CNN. Tell them I'm meeting with my top staff regarding the case and we'll call them back within the hour."

Tammy acknowledged the command, then closed her boss's door so they could have some peace and quiet.

"Top staff?" Brunelle laughed. "I like that."

"Don't get a big head," Duncan replied. "It sounded better than I have to talk to the prosecutor who's gonna get stuck with this case."

Brunelle smiled. "Yeah, that does sound less impressive."

Duncan shook his head and came out from behind his desk. He and Brunelle sat at the conference table where Duncan preferred to have his conversations with his prosecutors. "The national media is all over this. They're calling it the Seattle Sex Club Killing. What the hell happened?"

Brunelle shrugged. "Master Michael got a little careless with his knot-tying and choked out his sub."

Duncan just blinked at him several times. "What?"

Brunelle had to laugh. "Yeah, that was kinda my reaction too," he said. "Apparently the victim and the killer were boyfriend-girlfriend and into bondage. He tied her up too tight and she choked to death."

"Was it intentional?"

"Didn't look like it," Brunelle replied. "I listened to him tell his story to the cops and he sure sounded remorseful."

Duncan frowned and looked away. "Damn it," he finally said.

"What?" Brunelle wondered what was bothering his boss so much.

"I'm not looking forward to explaining why we didn't file charges," Duncan answered. "Even to CNN."

But Brunelle raised his palms. "Well, don't decline charges just yet. I said he sounded remorseful. That doesn't mean he truly was. For all we know, he planned the whole thing and was ready for his sob story. Kat—er, the medical examiner—probably hasn't even done the autopsy yet. Maybe there's a different cause of death. Maybe he just used the bondage to cover it up. It's too soon to tell."

Duncan nodded and his spirits visibly lifted. "Okay, okay. Good point." Then his mouth twisted in thought. "When's the autopsy?"

Brunelle wasn't sure he liked where this was going. "Uh, I'm not sure. Sometime this morning. I doubt she's started yet."

"Good," Duncan replied. "Call your girlfriend and tell her to wait until you get there. I want you to observe the autopsy and make sure she looks for signs of foul play."

Brunelle laughed. "Did you really just say, 'foul play'?"

Duncan grinned. "I'm old school. So sue me. Some guy chokes his girlfriend to death, I want to file charges. I don't care if it was some sick sex game. You don't kill people. Not in my county."

"Atta boy, Matt," Brunelle offered. "Don't let a little thing like kinky sex between consenting adults get between you and a murder charge."

But Duncan shook his head. "I don't want a murder charge. I want a murder conviction. Under the court rules, we can hold this guy seventy-two hours before we have to charge him or let him go. Go to the autopsy, then call the lead detective and tell him to look for anything to suggest these two were having problems. Friends, family, fellow perverts. Whatever. Then we staff this thing tomorrow afternoon and make a decision. I can hold off the media until then."

"Staff it?" Brunelle asked. Staffing it meant a conference table surrounded by senior prosecutors, debating and deciding what to do with the case. Brunelle hated staffings. He got paid to make decisions; he didn't need other people's opinions getting in his way.

"Absolutely," Duncan replied. "If I'm going to go on camera to explain what we're doing with this case, it's damn well going to be after we've discussed every possible contingency."

Brunelle nodded, but didn't reply. He knew better than to argue, because he knew Duncan was probably right.

"It'll be you and me," Duncan went on, a thoughtful finger raised to his lips. "And Fletcher and Jurgens." He thought for a minute. "And Yamata. I want her here too."

"Michelle Yamata?" Brunelle questioned. He liked her well enough, but still thought of her as a junior prosecutor. "Isn't she kinda new for this?"

Duncan shrugged, but smiled. "You tried a homicide with her. You said she did a good job. And she did a good job handling your cases when you took that leave of absence."

Brunelle frowned. That was all true.

"Besides," Duncan ignored the frown, "we need her."

Brunelle raised an eyebrow. "We do?"

"Yes," Duncan replied. "Before we make a decision on this one, I want to hear what a woman thinks about the whole thing."

Brunelle nodded. *Good idea.* Which reminded him. "Speaking of which, I better get going." He stood up to leave. "I'll go see what our lady medical examiner thinks about it."

CHAPTER 4

"Lady medical examiner?" Kat repeated back with a tight laugh. "It sounds like the girls teams at a high school. The Lady Vikings or something."

Brunelle laughed. "I don't think there were lady Vikings," he said. "I mean, if there were any female Vikings, they probably weren't very ladylike."

"Still," Kat crossed her arms and leaned against the examining table which was awaiting the remains of Christina Belfair, "you don't call the women in your office 'lady prosecutors.'"

"Prosecutrix," Brunelle offered.

"Excuse me?" Kat laughed at the word. "Prosecutrix? That's not a real word."

But Brunelle smiled and nodded. "Oh yes it is. Or it was. You see it in old case opinions sometimes. It's kind of a cool word."

Kat lowered her eyelids. "Sounds kinda dirty."

Brunelle offered an inappropriate leer. "I know."

Kat laughed at his exaggerated expression. "Well, then I wanna be a medical examintrix, or something."

Brunelle laughed. "Or something," he said. "Okay. I bet we

can come up with a title that ends in –trix."

Kat didn't laugh in response. Instead she sized up her boyfriend for moment. "Oh yeah?"

Brunelle felt the blush that Kat could always evoke in him rise into cheeks. But he could still function. "Yeah," he said. "Maybe."

Then Kat pushed herself off the metal table and stepped over to Brunelle. She grabbed his tie, but instead of tightening it like a leash, she wrapped it loosely around her wrist. "And what if that's not what I want, Mr. Brunelle?" she purred.

Brunelle might have blushed again, except his blood was rushing in the exact opposite direction.

"Ahem," coughed the technician who was rolling in the body for the autopsy. "Sorry to interrupt," she said. "Here's your next one, doctor."

Nothing breaks the mood quite like a dead body. Kat let go of Brunelle's tie and got back to business. She unzipped the body bag, then she and the technician lifted the remains from the gurney to the examining table. All of the clothes—and restraints—were still on.

"You gonna watch from in here?" Kat asked.

Brunelle shook his head. He was used to the smell, but that didn't mean he liked it. "No. Duncan said I had to watch, but he didn't say I had to be in the room." He jerked a thumb toward the large window on the opposite wall. "I'll watch from the observation room. Grab a cup a coffee and admire your skills."

Kat looked at him over her shoulder, which only accentuated those curves of hers he liked so much, "You sure it's my skills you'll be admiring?"

"I didn't say that was all I'd be admiring." He actually kissed her on the cheek in front of the technician—a rare public display of affection for him—and turned toward the observation room. Kat covered her cheek with a gloved hand and watched after him, shaking her head, but smiling.

* * *

A little less than an hour later, Kat came into the observation room to join Brunelle. The autopsy was finished and Brunelle poured her a cup of coffee while she pulled off and discarded her gloves in the bio-hazard bin.

"Definitely asphyxiation," Kat reported as she took the steaming mug from Brunelle. "Mostly strangulation, but the gag in her mouth didn't help matters."

"All the rope and shit probably didn't help matters either," Brunelle opined.

"Yes and no," Kat answered. "The arm-sleeve actually probably helped a bit. You put your arms back like that and it really opens your airways."

Brunelle nodded. He liked that she knew things he didn't know she knew. He wondered if it was purely medical knowledge.

"And the collar may actually have helped too," Kat added.

Brunelle raised an eyebrow. "Collar?"

Kat laughed at his eyebrow. "Yes. A nice leather one. Full inch wide. It even had a nametag that said 'Precious.'"

"A nametag?" Brunelle confirmed. "Like a dog?"

Kat shook her head. "No, like a submissive. And like I said, it may have helped. The rope was too constrictive, but the collar was rigid. It probably kept the rope from choking her out right away. In a way, that's sort of what killed her."

Brunelle cocked his head. "How do you mean?"

"The open airways from the arm-sleeve and the protection from strangulation from the collar delayed and disguised her respiratory distress. She was probably fine when the gag went in, but by the time she couldn't get enough air, she couldn't say anything."

Brunelle frowned and set down his coffee. "Well, that sucks."

Kat nodded, but drank from hers. "That would be a scary way to go."

But Brunelle shook his head. "No, I mean it sucks for me. I don't know what to do with Master Michael. He killed his girlfriend, but you're telling me it was an accident."

Kat raised a finger. "I never said it was an accident. And accident is when a construction crane falls on you. This was homicide. She died because of what another person did to her."

Brunelle took some solace in that answer, but not much. "Well, it doesn't sound like there was any intent, so it wasn't murder."

"There's no intent when a drunk driver kills grandma in the crosswalk," Kat retorted, "but that doesn't mean it's not a crime."

Brunelle chewed his cheek for a moment, then leaned forward and kissed Kat's cheek again. "You're right. You're absolutely right."

CHAPTER 5

"Manslaughter?" Joe Fletcher practically spat from his seat across Duncan's conference table. "That's chicken shit, Brunelle. Either charge murder or don't charge anything."

Brunelle really didn't like Fletcher. He never really had, but they'd basically been able to avoid each other over the years. Different divisions, different assignments, different cases. He was a good attorney, had a lot of experience, and won most of his cases. He was just a jerk.

"It's not chicken shit," Brunelle replied evenly, "to charge the proper crime. Manslaughter in the first degree fits the best."

But Fletcher shook his head exaggeratedly. "No, manslaughter is when you point a gun at your buddy's face, you think it's unloaded so you pull the trigger, and you blow his brains all over your wall. That's manslaughter. This is two perverts. Either he wanted her dead and used the bondage stuff to cover it up, or she just struggled too much and ended up dead."

Brunelle didn't immediately reply. He had also considered that angle. Sticks and stones break my bones, but whips and chains cover up premeditation.

The rest of the room also considered Fletcher's summation.

Duncan was sitting in the corner, leaning away from the table, hand over his mouth in concentration. Yamata was sitting at the table, hands folded, the junior member of the team apparently waiting her turn. And Paul Jurgens' large frame creaked in his chair as he leaned forward, breathing audibly, to join the conversation.

"Dave," he started with a wheeze. He was the oldest one in the room, balding, and way too overweight. He'd been at the office before even Duncan, but with no political or leadership aspirations, he had settled in trying major crimes and being asked his opinion. He was pretty jaded anymore, but he carried in an affable way. "Did your detective find anything to suggest premeditation? Problems in the relationship? Financial difficulties? Another woman? Any texts or emails or new life insurance policies?"

And that was why Fletcher was wrong. "No." Brunelle shook his head. "Nothing. All indications are they were a happy couple."

"Except for the rope around her throat," Fletcher scoffed.

"That doesn't necessarily mean anything," Yamata piped in. "Probably just the opposite."

Fletcher raised an eyebrow at the attractive prosecutor. "You into that shit too?"

Yamata grinned. "Don't even think it, Joe. You'd be the one in handcuffs."

Duncan leaned forward and coughed loudly. "All right, all right. I understand there's a sexual component to this homicide, but let's keep it professional. No one wants to get sued."

Brunelle smiled and looked at Yamata, who had to grin too. She'd been a lawyer with a civil firm before she sued them for sexual discrimination. The rumor mill had turned that into a suit for sexual harassment and half the prosecutor's office was scared to say boo to her. Brunelle would have given Fletcher credit for not being afraid of her, but really he was just dense. But Duncan was right to keep the off-color remarks to a minimum. There would be enough of those as the case progressed.

"Fine," Yamata acquiesced. "My point is, there seems to be no evidence of intent to harm and plenty of evidence that their activities were… consensual. I don't see us being able to prove murder."

"So chalk it up as a freak accident," Fletcher said. "And I do mean freak. Isn't there something about assumption of risk? You let some pervert tie you up like that you might end up dead. This probably happens all the time."

Brunelle shook his head. "I don't think so. We've got national media crawling up our asses, right, Matt? If this happened a lot, we'd all know about it."

Duncan nodded. "Everybody from our local affiliates to CNN wants an interview. Once we make our decision, we better be able to explain it in a simple sound bite. I don't want to get into the complexities of this kind of weird sexual relationship."

"But that's the problem," Yamata said. "The complexities drive the decision. As much I hate to admit it, Fletcher kind of has a point."

Fletcher crossed his arms and nodded. "Of course I do."

Yamata shook her head. "You don't even know your point."

Fletcher's smug smile faded. "Yes, I do," he insisted unconvincingly.

"What's his point?" Brunelle asked Yamata.

"To the extent that our victim consented to the restraints," Yamata said, "it will be hard to show any criminal liability by the defendant."

"He's not a defendant yet," Jurgens interrupted. "He's only a defendant if we charge him. Let's call him the suspect."

"Let's call him the killer," Brunelle retorted. "Tina's dead because Master Michael killed her. She doesn't die without his actions."

There were a few moments of silence, then Yamata raised an eyebrow. "Master Michael?"

Brunelle rolled his eyes, but had to laugh. "Yeah. That's his stage name, or whatever. But the point is, the victim is dead because of her lover's actions. He needs to be held responsible."

"It was an accident," Fletcher sneered. "Accidents aren't crimes."

But Jurgens shook his head. "They can be. What about vehicular homicide?"

"You get drunk and run somebody over, that's not an accident," Fletcher countered.

"You don't have to be drunk," Brunelle responded. "You can get charged with it just from driving recklessly."

"But that's a car," Fletcher insisted. "Not a rope and some handcuffs. You pull the trigger on a gun you think is unloaded and it's not, you're an idiot and you deserve to go to prison. But you tie up your perv girlfriend a little too tight? That's a mistake, not a crime. If there's no evidence he planned it to get rid of her, then I say we don't charge shit and Mister Michael walks."

"Master Michael," Brunelle corrected. He turned to Duncan. "What do you think, Matt? It's your call."

Duncan had been listening quietly to his prosecutors. He leaned forward onto the conference table. "What's your gut tell you, Dave? It's your case."

Brunelle thought for a moment. "It's not murder. He didn't intend to kill her. But it's not just an accident either. He should have known better. It was reckless, or at least negligent. You kill someone with criminal negligence, that's manslaughter."

Duncan nodded then looked around the table. "Joe, I know what you think. What about you, Paul?"

Jurgens shrugged. "I dunno. It kind of doesn't matter. She

isn't coming back no matter what we do."

Yep, thought Brunelle. *He's as jaded as they get.*

Duncan turned to Yamata. "Michelle?"

Yamata pursed her lips into a thoughtful frown then drummed her perfectly manicured fingernails on the conference table. "Like I said, Fletcher's got a point. This feels like an accident. But it was an avoidable one. That woman shouldn't be dead. I agree with Dave. It's manslaughter."

Duncan nodded. "Good. Then you're going to be second chair."

"Second chair?" Brunelle questioned even before Yamata could. "I don't need a second chair. I can handle a fucking manslaughter case by myself."

Then he remembered to look at Yamata. "No offense," he assured.

She laughed. "Oh, no. Of course not," she said sarcastically.

But Duncan was undeterred. "It may not be P.C. and I'll deny it to anyone who asks, especially the media, but you need a woman at the prosecutor's table with you. This is too sensitive to have it look like it's being prosecuted by some middle-aged man from the suburbs who doesn't know an arm-sleeve from a shirtsleeve."

Brunelle just blinked at him for several seconds. "I live in the city."

Yamata let out a small laugh. "That's your reply? Oh, yeah, you need me on this case."

"You're too vanilla," Duncan explained.

"Vanilla?" Brunelle repeated. "I don't even know what that means."

Yamata leaned over and patted him on the shoulder. "Exactly."

CHAPTER 6

Brunelle drafted up the complaint and supporting affidavit. One count of Manslaughter in the First Degree. Not murder, but still a homicide. Minimum seven years in prison, so serious stuff. Master Michael Atkins had spent two nights in the King County Jail. Under the court rules, Brunelle either had to charge or release him on day number three. So he scheduled the arraignment for 1:30 that afternoon, when he would formally file the charge. Usually the public defenders handled the arraignment, then the defendant could opt to hire his own attorney, although it wasn't unheard of for an attorney to be hired beforehand. When Brunelle answered his phone, it never even occurred to him that the attorney on the other end of the line had just been hired by Atkins.

"Hey, Dave!" gushed Nick Lannigan. "How's it going, man? Long time, no cases."

Lannigan had been a defense attorney in Seattle at least as long as Brunelle had been prosecuting there. But Lannigan didn't do homicide. He barely did any felonies at all. Maybe a car theft or simple drug possession for an existing client who got a new charge, but his business model was high volume misdemeanors: DUI, driving suspended, misdemeanor DV. Get in, get paid, get out. Not homicides.

"Hey, Nick," Brunelle replied. They'd gotten along well enough when Brunelle was still doing shoplifting cases. "Good to hear from you. What's up?"

"Well, actually, I'm calling about the Atkins case," Lannigan said. He sounded embarrassed to even say it.

Brunelle didn't know what to say. He was speechless. Was Atkins really that stupid?

"Dave?" Lannigan said after a moment. "Dave, you there?"

"Uh, yeah," Brunelle replied. "Yeah, I'm here. I'm just, uh, surprised, I guess. I didn't think you handled homicides."

Lannigan laughed. "I don't. But I handle money. This Atkins guy got referred to me. Do you know how much I can charge for a murder case? It's worth ten DUIs. Maybe twelve."

Brunelle nodded into the phone. He understood the business side of it. He'd overheard plenty of conversations in the courthouse hallways between defense attorneys discussing fee arrangements and 401(k)s and condos in Hawaii. But just because he knew about the money motive didn't mean he wanted to talk about it.

"I hope you got paid up front," Brunelle said, a bit cryptically.

"Oh, I did," Lannigan replied. "No way I'm touching this without half up front. I take credit cards, so he actually paid it. And it's non-refundable, so please tell me you're not filing charges. It'll be the easiest money I've ever made."

"We're not filing murder charges," Brunelle said with a grin.

"Woohoo!" Lannigan yelled. "Thank you, David Brunelle. I should give you a cut of the fee."

Brunelle ignored the completely unethical suggestion. He was eager to deliver the punch line. "We're filing manslaughter charges."

"What?!" Lannigan wailed. "Manslaughter? Are you

freaking kidding me?"

"Sorry, Nick," Brunelle lied. "Looks like you're going to have to earn that fee after all."

Lannigan hesitated then laughed again. He was a pretty genial guy. Brunelle liked him well enough—and he was confident he could pretty much wipe the courtroom floor with him. "I guess so," Lannigan conceded.

"The arraignment's at one-thirty," Brunelle informed him. "See you then."

Lannigan sighed. "Well, at least it's not a murder charge. I'm already ahead of the game."

"If you say so, Nick," Brunelle replied. "See you in court."

* * *

The cameras practically choked the hallway. So to speak. Brunelle shook his head at the metaphor that had popped into his head and strode toward the arraignment court.

"Hey, Dave." Several of the local cameramen and reporters greeted him as he approached. There were also some national guys Brunelle didn't recognize. The local guys knew he wouldn't comment until after the arraignment, and then only to offer a tepid sound bite about holding people responsible for their actions and having confidence in the strength of the evidence. But the national guys didn't care about the subtleties of criminal law or the ethical constraints on a prosecutor when addressing the media. They were there for one reason: sex sells.

"Mr. Prosecutor," one young blonde woman ran up to him, microphone extended and cameraman in tow, his spotlight blinding Brunelle momentarily. "Could you please comment on the bondage murder case? Will you be seeking the death penalty? Do you think the killer would enjoy it?"

Brunelle blinked at the reporter for a moment. It wasn't a death penalty case. It wasn't even a murder case. Enjoy being executed? What the hell was wrong with the media? But he bit his tongue. "I'll comment after the arraignment."

The woman ignored the brush off. "Could you just say something like, 'We have enough evidence to prove he's fifty shades of guilty'?"

"Fifty shades of guilty?" Brunelle couldn't help but repeat back, stunned by the phrase.

"Good," the reporter said, "but say it like a statement. That sounded like a question. We can't really use that."

Wow. Brunelle almost admired her tenacity. And her creativity. But he knew better than to try any case in the media. "I'll comment after the arraignment."

Then he broke off and headed for the courtroom door. One of the local guys opened the door for him, "Can we get copies of the charging docs after the arraignment?"

That was the standard operating procedure. Brunelle patted his file. "Got 'em right here. Thanks, Brian."

Brian the cameraman nodded and Brunelle stepped into the courtroom. There were more reporters inside and the one 'pool' camera the judges usually allowed. All the stations would share the footage. Brunelle passed through the secure door and into the forward part of the courtroom set off from the gallery by a wall of windows. The courtroom was used all day for felony arraignments, most of the defendants being in custody. It was far more secure to have the front part of the courtroom locked off than have to worry about every defendant thinking about making a break for it in a crowded courtroom. And when the microphones were off, Brunelle could speak his mind.

"What the fuck is wrong with those national reporters?" he asked Jessica Edwards, his counterpart at the King County Public Defender's Office. She was one of their top people and had apparently come down to handle the Atkins arraignment personally. She must not have heard from Lannigan yet. "Somebody's dead and they want me to say the defendant is 'fifty shades of guilty.'"

Edwards let out a laugh despite herself. "Oh, that's awesome. You gonna use that in your opening?"

"No way," Brunelle replied, setting his file down on the prosecutor's table. "And I'm not going to use the word 'opening' either. This case is going to be full of double entendres."

Edwards smiled. She was about the same age as Brunelle, with straight blonde hair and wise lines around her eyes. She would have been a much tougher adversary than Lannigan. Brunelle actually mourned the loss a bit. "Can I look at the paperwork before the judge comes out?" she asked.

Brunelle frowned. "Sorry. Atkins hired a private attorney. He's supposed to show to do the arraignment?"

Edwards' smile evaporated. Clearly she wanted to keep the case. It was going to be entertaining. It was also one the defense could actually win. "Who'd he hire?" she asked.

Brunelle tried to keep a poker face. "Nick Lannigan." He knew he'd failed.

"Nick?" Edwards asked, almost aghast. "He's not qualified to do a murder case."

Brunelle didn't disagree. "Well, good thing it's a manslaughter case then."

"Manslaughter?" Edwards asked. Then she thought for a moment and nodded. "That's a good call, Dave. You were gonna have a hell of a time proving intent."

"I know," Brunelle agreed. "I'm pretty sure I can prove recklessness. I saw her at the scene. The whole escapade looked pretty damn reckless."

"Don't knock it 'til you've tried it, Mr. B."

It was Robyn Dunn, one of the junior attorneys at the public defender's office. She looked as great as the last time Brunelle had seen her. Her auburn curls bounced on her shoulders as she walked over to him from the row of private attorney-inmate conference stalls. She had that same dimple on just one side of her face that popped when she was smiling, like right then. And she had that scar on her opposite cheek that she made no effort to conceal. "Long time no nothing," she said as she got one step too close to him. "Are you trying to avoid me?"

Brunelle wasn't very good at trying to avoid attractive women. "No, ma'am," he managed to reply without stammering. He was suddenly very glad Nick Lannigan, balding, middle aged man, was going to be the defense attorney.

"Ma'am?" Robyn giggled. "That would make me the dom, silly."

Brunelle just stared at her, uncertain how to respond. Robyn cocked an eyebrow at him, then turned to walk away. "I think you might want to do a little research before you try this case." She looked over her shoulder and lowered her eyelids. "Sir."

Brunelle felt a rush of blood go to several parts of his body, including his cheeks.

Edwards shook her head at him. "She's half your age, Dave."

Robyn had stepped out of the courtroom, so Brunelle felt at liberty to respond, "She's two-thirds of my age, thank you. And anyway, I have a girlfriend."

Edwards nodded. "Yes, I know," she said. "Dr. Death. Just you be sure to remember it too, good sir."

Again with the 'sir,' Brunelle thought. He needed to get on with the arraignment. "Where the hell is Nick?" he asked testily.

"Right here, right here," Lannigan answered as he scurried through the security door. "Sorry I'm late. I was giving an interview to one of the national reporters. It was kinda fun."

Brunelle rolled his eyes. "Can we just get on with this? I want to get back to my office."

He handed Lannigan copies of the charging paperwork.

Lannigan accepted them and scanned the top sheet. "We'll waive formal arraignment. Let's just set a pretrial hearing and get out of here."

Brunelle sighed. Edwards chuckled.

"You can't waive arraignment on a felony," Brunelle explained. "You can only do that on misdemeanors. Are you sure you're ready for this, Nick?"

Maybe there was still a chance for the defense team of Jessica Edwards and Robyn Dunn.

"I got paid," Lannigan replied, "so I guess I better be. I'll figure it out." He looked around. "Which table is for the defense attorney?"

* * *

Twenty minutes later, Master Michael had been brought into court handcuffed and wearing orange jail jammies decidedly less stylish than his leather and bare chest look of a few nights earlier. Lannigan had known enough to plead not guilty and the judge set bail at $100,000, standard on a manslaughter charge. There had been a titter through the gallery when it was revealed that the prosecution wouldn't be seeking a murder conviction, so Brunelle knew he was in for a grilling when he returned to the reporters in the hallway.

"Mr. Brunelle, Mr. Brunelle!" It was the blonde national reporter who elbowed her way to the front of the paparazzi in the hallway. "Why aren't you pursuing murder charges?"

Brunelle was prepared. "We reviewed all the available information and we charged Mr. Atkins with the crime we believe best fits the evidence."

The reporter's expression showed that she found his

explanation strange. "But we've been reporting this as the bondage murder case all week," she protested.

Brunelle nodded and smiled politely. "I know."

The reporter's eyebrow knitted together. "Well, can you give us a sound bite anyway? Maybe something like, 'It's manslaughter even if it's a woman' or something. Something catchy."

Brunelle held his smile. "We reviewed all the available information and we charged Mr. Atkins with the crime we believe best fits the evidence," he repeated. "Thank you."

He turned and walked toward the elevators. The reporter shouted another question after him but he knew he was ethically prohibited from saying anything other than the charges and that they had reviewed the evidence to arrive at those charges. Prosecutors weren't supposed to try cases in the media. But he wasn't thinking about her questions anyway.

He was thinking about research.

CHAPTER 7

"Research?" Kat asked over Brunelle's shoulder as he hastily spun his laptop away from her. "That's not research. That's porn."

Brunelle sat up straight in his seat at his dining room table where he'd set up a makeshift office and internet station. "I assure you, madam, this is for purely professional purposes."

"It's after hours and you're at home," Kat reminded him.

Brunelle laughed. "There's no way I could look at this stuff on my county computer. I'd get fired in an instant."

"Matt would never fire his Golden Boy," Kat returned. "Lemme see what you're looking at." She turned the laptop back around so they could both see the computer. "Oh my."

On the screen was an image of what likely would have happened that night between Master Michael and Tied-up Tina if Mikey hadn't ended up strangling her during the proceedings. A lithe young woman was kneeling on some sort of platform. She was wearing a combination of lingerie, leather, and bindings. Her movement was obviously restricted. Directly behind her stood her lover, his proximity leaving no doubt as to their current activity.

"Wow," breathed Kat after a few moments. "They do look like they're having fun."

Brunelle nodded, but didn't pull his eyes from the screen. "Yeah. Of course she's not being strangled to death."

Kat put a hand on Brunelle's shoulder. She gave it a squeeze and rub. "So you've been looking at a lot of this stuff?"

Brunelle shrugged, enjoying the weight of his lover's hand. "I guess so. There's a surprising amount of it. You should see the videos."

Kat squeezed his shoulder again, then ran her hand up to the base of his neck. "Videos? Yeah, maybe I should."

She let go of Brunelle's neck and picked up the laptop.

"What are you doing?" Brunelle asked.

But Kat ignored the question. She started walking toward Brunelle's bedroom. "Do you have any rope?"

"Rope?" Brunelle repeated. "Uh, no. Who has rope lying around?"

Kat nodded at the laptop screen. "I bet these two do." She smiled at him over her shoulder. "Well, no worries. You have lots of neckties, right?"

Brunelle finally stood up and started toward her. "What do you have in mind, Dr. Anderson?"

She reached out and grabbed his shirt, then lowered her eyelids and kissed his cheek. "Research."

CHAPTER 8

The next morning, Brunelle felt like a regular expert. His research assistant had helped greatly. But he was about to be reminded what he was truly an expert in, and what he wasn't. And that being an expert didn't always ensure making the right decision.

"Knock, knock." His legal assistant, Nicole, rapped gently on his door frame just before lunch. He'd been working all morning on a response to a motion to suppress the DNA results on another of his cases. He loved being in court, but he hated writing briefs. He welcomed the interruption. "Nick Lannigan is here to see you," said Nicole.

Brunelle smiled. Maybe Nick had come offering to plead the guy out and get the case over with. That was his usual m.o. "Great. I'll be right there."

"Is this on the BDSM case?" Nicole asked.

Brunelle cocked his head. "BD..?"

Nicole rolled her eyes, but smiled at him. "BDSM. Bondage, discipline, and sado-masochism," she explained. "The sex club case?"

Apparently Brunelle needed to do more research—at least on the terminology. But he smiled at the thought of his research partner and the neckties he couldn't wear again until they'd been to the dry cleaner's. "Right. Uh, yeah. That case."

He realized he might be blushing, so he changed the topic slightly. "Lannigan doesn't usually do homicides, so, ya know, I think he's a little in over his head."

Nicole gave Brunelle an appraising glance, then smiled again. "He's not the only one." Before Brunelle could react, she turned away. "I'll go get him."

Brunelle frowned at Nicole's comment but before he could think of the come-back he should have given, Lannigan was rolling into his office, hand extended and face grinning. "Dave, great to see you again. Sorry about dropping in unannounced."

Brunelle shook the defense attorney's hand and they sat down across from each other over Brunelle's desk. "No problem," Brunelle replied. He gestured toward his computer monitor. "I needed a break from this brief anyway."

"Great, great," Lannigan answered. "Well, I'll get right to it. I think you should cut my guy a reckless endangerment. He'll plead to that today and we can both get on with our other cases."

"Reckless endangerment?" Brunelle repeated. He shook his head. "That's a misdemeanor. No way, Nick. I'm not cutting your guy a misdemeanor. He killed someone."

Lannigan shrugged. "It was an accident."

"I know," Brunelle agreed. "That's why it's manslaughter. Accident plus dead body equals manslaughter. If it was intentional, it'd be murder."

Lannigan shifted in his seat and put his nervous hands together in a sort of wringing prayer position. "Look, reckless endangerment fits. It's doing something recklessly that puts people in danger. That's what happened here."

"If she'd only been injured, I might agree with you," Brunelle replied. "But she's dead. Reckless endangerment is for stupid shit like shooting a gun off on New Year's Eve, not strangling your lover to death."

Lannigan wasn't a very good negotiator. "But it was an accident," he repeated, almost whining.

Brunelle nodded, almost patiently. "Right. That's why it's manslaughter."

Lannigan pursed his lips and looked away. "I thought you'd be more reasonable, Dave. Hasn't my guy suffered enough? He lost the love of his life."

"He killed the love of his life," Brunelle corrected. "And I'm not really interested in how much he's suffered. He broke the law."

"What about mercy?" Lannigan pleaded.

"Not to be clichéd," Brunelle answered, "but tell it to the judge. My job is to obtain the conviction for what he did. He did manslaughter. The judge gives mercy, or not, at sentencing. Why not just plead him out as charged, and make a pitch to the judge for leniency? He's more likely to get a light sentence if he accepts responsibility."

Lannigan chewed his cheek for a moment. His usually genial expression clouded by a furrowed brow and hesitant frown. Then his features snapped back to the amiable mask he wore. "I know! *You* talk to him."

Brunelle's eyebrows shot up. "Me? I don't talk to the defendants. That's your job."

But Lannigan shook his head. "No, he won't listen to me. I've tried to explain why he's gonna get convicted, but he doesn't want to hear it. He figures he hired me for something and not just to plead guilty. He could do that without me."

"He hired you for legal advice," Brunelle replied. "And you should advise him to plead guilty."

"Yeah, well..." Lannigan trailed off for a bit. "I'm not sure he trusts my advice."

Brunelle just nodded, in a way he hoped was noncommittal.

"He only hired me because I quoted such a low fee," Lannigan admitted. "Half what everybody else charges for a homicide." He reached up and rubbed the back of his neck. "Shit, Dave, I didn't think you'd actually charge it. It was an accident."

Brunelle folded his hands on his desk. "Yeah, we've been through that." He frowned for a moment, then leaned forward. "Look, Nick, it's not really my problem if your client doesn't trust you because you low-balled the fee. The truth is, there were plenty of people in my office who thought we should charge murder. But I charged manslaughter because it was manslaughter. And that's what he needs to plead to."

Lannigan nodded. "So tell him that," he practically begged. "He'll listen to you."

Brunelle shook his head. "Nick, you know I can't talk to defendants. Not directly. The rules of professional conduct forbid it. I don't need that kind of hassle."

But Lannigan waved it off. "It's okay if I'm there. I'll set it up. I'll tell him you won't budge and I'll let you explain why."

Brunelle raised steepled fingers to his lips. "I don't know, Nick. Why should I do that?"

Lannigan's face lit up. "Easy, Dave. We both get rid of another case. Don't you have enough to do?"

Brunelle glanced again at the suppression brief on his computer. He'd do almost anything to avoid going back to that. He tapped his chin. "You think it'll work? You think he'll plead out if I explain how strong our case is?"

Lannigan nodded enthusiastically—a defense attorney bobblehead. "Absolutely. I guarantee it."

Brunelle didn't believe the guarantee, but he figured the whole thing was worth a shot. "You'll be there the whole time, right?"

More exaggerated nods. He could tell he'd won Brunelle over. "You bet."

"And no questions," Brunelle insisted. "I don't want him asking me questions. I explain it and he decides. That's it."

Lannigan stood up and stuck his hand across Brunelle's desk. "Deal."

Brunelle looked at the hand dubiously, then shrugged and shook it. "Okay. Set it up. But if he doesn't plead out, I'm asking for the maximum sentence."

Lannigan smiled. "Sure, Dave. Whatever you say."

But Brunelle could feel he'd already said too much.

CHAPTER 9

Somehow, when Brunelle had accepted Lannigan's offer, he'd pictured himself meeting with Master Michael in one of the small attorney-client conference rooms inside the jail. But he'd forgotten that bail was a lot lower on a manslaughter charge than murder, and Michael Atkins wasn't some gangbanger or drug addict. He had a respectable job and a mortgage. He wasn't a thug, just a pervert. Once the judge set the bail, it took Lannigan less than a day to set up a bail bond, secured by his client's suburban home. So the meeting was at Lannigan's office, and Atkins was wearing khakis and a button-up shirt rather than jail jammies or leather pants. He stood up when Brunelle walked into the conference room that Lannigan shared with the other small time attorneys on the floor.

"Mr. Brunelle." Atkins extended a hand in greeting. "Nick says I should talk to you."

Brunelle shook his hand. He didn't like how Michael had phrased that. "He told me the same thing."

Lannigan jumped in, directing Atkins back into his seat and gesturing for Brunelle to sit opposite. Lannigan sat between them, at the head of the table. "Thanks for coming, Dave," he started, talking a bit quickly. "I just thought it might be a good idea to lay everything out on the table and see if we can't just work this all out."

Atkins nodded and looked to Brunelle. "I'm guessing you don't understand my and Tina's relationship. It wasn't abusive."

Brunelle nodded back, but it was noncommittal, designed to elicit additional information rather than ratify that already provided. "Okay."

Atkins grimaced slightly at the response. "See, that tells me you don't understand. Most vanillas don't. But don't judge me. I'm sure you're tolerant of gays, and May-December relationships, and I'm guessing by your bare ring finger that you understand polyamory."

Brunelle knew gay people, and he thought he'd heard the term 'May-December relationship' once about a decade earlier. He had no idea what polyamory was. But none of those was the term he fixated on.

"Vanillas?" he asked.

Atkins smiled and nodded. "Right. People like you who don't get people like me and Tina. It's fine if you want to do it in the default position twice a month, but that doesn't work for everyone."

It was like Atkins was speaking in code. A rude, snarky code.

"The default position?" Brunelle questioned.

Atkins laughed slightly. "That's what Tina and I called the missionary position. The default position. But there's so much more. And for two people who enjoy the same play, from complimentary angles—oh, you have no idea how perfect and rare that is. It's not like I went to that club and picked up the first sub I saw. Tina and I met a long time ago. We both joined the same hiking club. It took a while until we realized how compatible we were sexually, but then... Well, I can't explain it."

Brunelle wasn't thrilled about being called a vanilla who only did it in the default position. For a moment he even considered telling Atkins and Lannigan just how non-vanilla he and Kat had been the previous night. But two things stopped him. First and foremost, Kat would have killed him. Slowly. In a way no one would have been able to detect. Second, he felt a bit intimidated by the Master and wondered if he might laugh at Brunelle's undoubtedly clumsy imitation of his lifestyle. So he turned prosecutorial.

"You better explain it," Brunelle responded. "You're looking at prison time for what you did."

"Prison?" Atkins' eyes widened. "You want to put me in prison?"

Brunelle shrugged. "You're putting yourself there, Mr. Atkins. You killed someone."

"I killed the woman I loved," Atkins replied sharply. "Isn't that punishment enough?"

Brunelle thought for a moment, then shook his head. "The legislature doesn't think so."

Atkins crossed his arms and scowled. "Then fuck the legi—"

But Lannigan interrupted him. "I think we're getting a bit off track here, fellas. What matters most is that this was an accident. Just a tragic accident. No one wanted to kill anyone that night, least of all my client wanting to kill the love of his life."

"Accidents happen," Brunelle agreed. "And sometimes those accidents are crimes. Manslaughter is, by definition, an accident. But it's still a crime, with a minimum seven years in prison." He shrugged and met Atkins' gaze. "Sorry," he lied.

Actually, it wasn't a lie. It's not a lie if you know the other person won't believe you.

"I'm not going to prison for seven years," Atkins declared.

Brunelle raised an eyebrow. Master Michael had been a

blubbering mess that night at the Cu-CUM-ber club. Brunelle had found it difficult to imagine Atkins mastering anyone. But now he was showing a bit of his inner control freak. *Good.* If Lannigan was stupid enough to put him on the stand, Brunelle would make sure the jury saw it too.

And Brunelle figured Lannigan was all but certain to put Atkins on the stand. Usually, defendants didn't help themselves. Good attorneys knew how to get their side of the story to the jury without exposing their client to the destructive force of a cross examination by the prosecutor. But Lannigan wasn't a good attorney.

"You may not have a lot of choice in the matter," Brunelle said. Then he decided to poke the bull. "How does it feel to have someone else in control?"

The good news was, Brunelle was enjoying himself. The bad news was, that wasn't why he was there. He was there to explain to Atkins why he was going to get convicted, and thus convince him to accept responsibility.

Lannigan could also see it wasn't going the way he'd envisioned. "Look, maybe we should start over," he said. He turned to his client. "I wanted you to meet Mr. Brunelle because he's a good and honest lawyer and he doesn't lay on the bullshit. He'll tell it like it is, and maybe he'll point out some weaknesses in our case that we can't see."

Atkins frowned and looked at Brunelle, then back to his lawyer. "I'm not sure I want to discuss the weaknesses in our case in front of the prosecutor. That doesn't seem smart."

Brunelle couldn't help but nod slightly. He was right; it wasn't smart. Brunelle could see Atkins was the more intelligent of the two other men in the room. He guessed Atkins knew it too. He was sure Lannigan knew it.

Time to cut to the chase.

"Look," Brunelle leaned forward and folded his hands on the conference table. "I'll make this easy. Don't say anything, just listen. Nick asked me to explain why I'm so damn confident you're going to get convicted. He figured if you heard it from me, you might believe it. Then you two could decide on your defense strategy. So, here goes.

"You said it was an accident. I get that. In fact, that's the first thing I'm going to tell the jury. 'Ladies and gentleman, this was an accident. A horrible, terrible, and preventable accident. It was also a crime.' See, that's the point. You get behind the wheel of a car drunk and kill someone, that's an accident too. You didn't intend to kill anyone. You just had a reckless disregard for the safety of others. That's not murder. It's manslaughter. Same here. You didn't mean to kill Tina, but you did, and you need to be held responsible."

Atkins twisted his mouth into a tight frown.

"Do you understand?" Lannigan asked him.

Atkins just narrowed his eyes for a moment, then started nodding. "Yeah, I understand. I understand perfectly." He stood up. "You got your money and now you want me to plead guilty. Well, fuck that. I'm not a criminal and I'm not going to prison. You're fired, Lannigan."

Lannigan's jaw dropped almost as far as Brunelle's heart.

No, I need Lannigan on this case. He'll make sure there's a conviction.

Lannigan popped out of his seat. "Now, Mike, Mike, Mike. Let's talk about this." He threw a nervous glance at Brunelle then turned back to his client. "Don't be hasty. This was just an idea. We can talk more. Alone."

Brunelle knew his cue to leave. He stood. "Nice to meet you, Mr. Atkins." Another non-lie, since Atkins wouldn't believe that either. He winked at Lannigan. "Good luck, Nick. Give me a call once you get this settled. I'll show myself out."

He started to do just that, when he remembered one more term of art that had been bothering him. He turned back.

"One more question, Mr. Atkins," Brunelle said. "What's polyamory?"

Atkins hesitated, momentarily distracted from his anger at Lannigan. "It means being in love with more than one person at the same time," he explained. "Can you even understand that?"

Brunelle nodded. Unfortunately, he could.

CHAPTER 10

Courthouses are small places. To be sure, they're usually large buildings, ten stories tall or sprawling over a city block, with a hundred courtrooms, and literally thousands of people passing through them each week. But the core group of lawyers and court staff who were there every day—they're a small group. Brunelle learned in school that nothing could travel faster than light. He learned in the courthouse that there was one exception: gossip.

By the time Brunelle passed through the metal detectors the next day, his little tête-a-tête with Master Michael was the talk of the place. But he was too distracted to notice whether anyone was looking sideways at him. His mind was racing over the events of the last twenty-four hours. Atkins' threat to fire Lannigan. Terms like 'vanilla' and 'polyamory.' Kat almost catching him as he googled 'polyamory' at his kitchen table. Distracting Kat from further 'Whatcha doing?' questions by leading her to his bedroom for more research. And the paradoxical feeling of satisfaction and increased curiosity said research was budding in him.

In fact, he was so preoccupied that he walked right past Robyn Dunn on his way to the elevators.

But she saw him.

"Hiya, Mr. B," she called out in that darkly sweet voice of hers. "Whatcha doing?"

Brunelle swung around, all of the thoughts in his head spilling onto the floor and bouncing away. Well, almost all of the thoughts.

"Uh, hey, Robyn," he stammered. That dimple. That damn dimple of hers. It looked good beneath leather. And he bet that it looked even better in the flesh — so to speak. "Just lost in thought, I guess. Big case."

Robyn smiled, which just deepened the dimple. The scar on the other side of her face had faded in color but not size. Her smile made it stretch slightly into its own smile shape. Brunelle estimated it was higher up her face enough to be hidden under the mask. He wondered how recent that photograph was.

He wondered if she still had the mask.

"The sex club case, right?" she guessed. "Yeah, everybody's talking about it."

Brunelle raised his eyebrows. "Oh yeah?"

Robyn nodded. "Sure. Guy offs his sub and is facing a manslaughter rap? That's way more interesting that some tweaker with meth in his pocket."

"I suppose so," Brunelle agreed.

"Besides," Robyn added. "Nick won't shut up about it. His guy fired him and he's pissed."

Damn it, Brunelle thought. *That pisses me off too.*

"He probably shouldn't do that," Brunelle replied. "Attorney-client confidences and all that. He doesn't need the Bar coming after him."

But Robyn waved the suggestion away. "Naw, Nick's not stupid," she started.

Brunelle wasn't so sure, but he managed to keep a poker face.

"He just told us the shit that wasn't protected. Like where his guy waived attorney-client privilege or something."

Brunelle nodded. "Okay," he said absently. If Lannigan was off the case, that meant Atkins was going to get an upgrade at attorney. Brunelle was more interested in who the new attorney would be than in whatever Lannigan had been going around telling people.

"You seem distracted, Dave," Robyn said. She reached out and took him by the elbow—which only succeeded in distracting him more. Her hand was so warm—and strong. She turned him toward the coffee cart at the other end of the lobby. "Let me buy you a coffee."

Brunelle wasn't about to decline. For one thing, he could use a coffee. For another, Robyn still had a hold of his arm.

"So yeah, anyway," she said as Brunelle went through the possible attorneys in his head. Herschel. Clausen. Moser. All the experienced, expensive ones the juries seemed to love. The case was going to be difficult enough. He didn't need a worthy opponent reminding the jury that sometimes accidents just happen. "Did you know," Robyn went on, "the most common way for an attorney-client communication to be not privileged is to have a third party in the room?"

Brunelle nodded. "Sure. Right." He didn't really worry too much about that attorney-client stuff. He didn't have a client. Not a flesh-and-blood one, anyway. His client was the State of Washington, whatever that meant.

They'd reached the coffee cart. Brunelle looked up at the menu board. *Maybe a mocha,* he thought, but Robyn interrupted his selection process.

"Let me order for you," she said.

He looked down at her, a bit perplexed. He tried to recall if they'd ever had coffee together before. "Do you know what I like?"

Again, that smile of hers, but combined with lowered eyelids that sent his blood rushing again. "I think so," she practically purred. She turned to the barista. "The gentleman will have a vanilla latte," she announced.

Brunelle cocked his head. "Vanilla latte? I don't like vanilla—"

"That's not what I heard," Robyn interrupted with a laugh.

The blood that had been rushing redirected itself straight to his cheek. And realizing he was blushing just made him even more embarrassed. And angry. "Wow," was all he could manage to say. He spun away and headed back to the elevators.

"Oh, come on, Dave!" Robyn yelled after him. "It was only a joke."

But he didn't turn around. He didn't like being teased. And he didn't like being mad at her. Especially because it just made him want her that much more.

CHAPTER 11

Not usually prone to being moody (at least if you asked him) Brunelle felt strangely out of balance when he got to his desk. Still angry and embarrassed by Robyn's little joke, he walked right past Nicole without saying hello and threw himself into his desk chair. Nicole knew his moods well enough and left him alone. He just needed time to focus and work and let the feelings burn away. The last thing he needed was a phone call from Master Michael's new attorney.

"Hello?" he answered the phone brusquely, eschewing his normal 'Prosecutor's Office, Dave Brunelle' greeting.

"Uh, hello," came the deep male voice on the other end. "I was trying to reach David Brunelle."

That shook Brunelle out of his funk. No reason to let his professionalism drop. "This is Dave Brunelle."

"Ah, Mr. Brunelle," came the reply. "I'm glad I reached you. This is Ron Jacobsen." Then, as if Brunelle should recognize it, "Of Smith, Lundquist, Jacobsen and Brown."

Brunelle had heard of 'Smith Lundquist.' They were one of the dozen or so mid-sized law firms in Seattle. Most of them were what was known as 'corporate firms,' meaning their clients tended to be corporations and their practice tended to be civil. Most criminal defense attorneys were solo practitioners, or maybe in a small two or three person partnership. So, while Brunelle had heard of Smith Lundquist, he'd never given much thought to the attorneys in the firm, let alone the other names on the front door. Now he was talking to one of them.

"Mr. Jacobsen," Brunelle feigned familiarity. "Nice to hear from you. What can I do for you?" Maybe, Brunelle thought, they were suing somebody and needed a copy of the police reports. But no such luck.

"I'm calling regarding the Michael Atkins case. Mr. Atkins just hired our firm to represent him in the criminal case against him. It's my understanding you're the prosecutor assigned to his case."

Brunelle sighed, but hoped not too loudly. So much for Nick Lannigan. *Damn.*

"That's right," he confirmed. "It's my case."

"Oh good," Jacobsen replied, his grin audible over the phone line. "Now I know who to serve with our motions."

"Motions?" Brunelle asked. He hated motions. Criminal law was about trials, not motions. Either the defendant robbed the store, shot the other guy, stole the car, or not. Bring in the witnesses, have them tell their stories, and let the jury decide. The only time motions were important was in drug cases where if the defense couldn't suppress the drugs for an unlawful search it was going to be pretty hard to convince the jury that the crack in the defendant's pocket wasn't his. But Brunelle wasn't in the drug unit; he was in homicide. Dead bodies and long trials. But not motions. Please, God, not motions. "What kind of motions?"

"All kinds of motions, Mr. Brunelle," Jacobsen answered gleefully. The corporate lawyers were all about motions practice. That's how they settled cases: overwhelming the other side with motions. Motions to compel discovery, motions to resist discovery, motions for subpoenas, motions to quash subpoenas, motions to dismiss, dissuade, disembowel. "This case cries out for several motions, the first of which is to modify my client's conditions of release."

"His conditions of release?" Brunelle questioned. "But he already posted bail. He's out. What needs to be changed?"

"It's not just about money, Mr. Brunelle," Jacobsen replied. Ironic, considering he was being paid to say that. "You've also restricted his movements unnecessarily and unjustly."

Brunelle tried to recall what the conditions were besides the dollar amount Atkins had to post to get out of jail. There was nothing special that he recalled. Just the usual stuff: no contact with witnesses, stay away from the crime scene, show up for court dates, don't leave the state. "How did we do that?"

"Why, Mr. Brunelle, I'm surprised," Jacobsen teased. "Don't you read the orders you obtain from the judge?"

Brunelle shrugged to himself. "Of course I do. But I don't always remember them. How exactly did we unjustly restrict your client's movements? Does he want to travel out of state?"

"Not at all," was the reply. "He wants to go back to the Cu-CUM-ber Club."

"But that's the crime scene," Brunelle protested reflexively.

"And that assumes there was a crime," Jacobsen pointed out. "Shame on you, Mr. Brunelle. You know my client is presumed innocent."

"Presumed innocent doesn't mean innocent in fact," Brunelle countered, growing increasingly irritated by Jacobsen's smugness. "Every defendant is ordered to stay away from the crime scene."

"But not every defendant has hired Smith, Lundquist, Jacobsen and Brown."

Brunelle felt grateful for that. "Right. Aren't you guys a civil firm? Why are you coming in on a criminal case?"

"We have a white collar crime team," Jacobsen explained.

Brunelle rolled his eyes. That was how corporate lawyers excused handling criminal cases, lest the good people of the world think they were as lowly as the prosecutors and defense attorneys who lined the gutters outside the courthouse. "Manslaughter isn't a white collar crime," he pointed out.

"But Mr. Atkins is a white collar client," Jacobsen replied. "He has a good job—"

"He must," Brunelle interrupted, "to hire you." He immediately regretted the remark.

"Well, yes," Jacobsen answered. "That is how it works. We can't all draw a government check, Mr. Brunelle."

Brunelle considered arguing the merits of public service versus private practice, but decided to forego the argument. At least for right then.

Jacobsen filled the silence. "Our motion to modify Mr. Atkins' conditions of release will be delivered to your office this afternoon. We'll note it for a hearing pursuant to the court rules."

How professional, Brunelle thought. The court rules would give him five court days to prepare for the hearing. Even so, he preferred the collegiality of Jessica Edwards calling him mid-afternoon to tell him she'd scheduled the bail hearing for the next morning, knowing he might have to do the same to her sometime on a later case. "Great."

"We'll be filing several more motions in the coming days, Mr. Brunelle." Jacobsen's words were half way between information and threat. "Please keep in mind that we don't accept service by email for your responses."

Brunelle shook his head. If he ever needed to be reminded why he should thank God he did criminal law, he just needed to lock horns occasionally with a civil lawyer. "Duly noted." Then he decided to provide his own information and threat. "You know, Ron," a little familiarity to catch his attention, "I'm not like the civil attorneys you usually go against. I don't have a client who's going to run out of money to reply to all of your frivolous motions."

Jacobsen actually seemed to enjoy Brunelle's little bit of aggression. "Of course not. But, Mr. Brunelle, I bill hourly. The more work I do, the more I get paid. You don't get paid one penny more no matter how much extra work I pile onto you." He paused. "Unless, you'd like to talk settlement. My client has authorized me to accept an offer of a misdemeanor."

Brunelle let out a small laugh. "I've been threatened with a lot worse than a pile of paper. I'll look forward to your abusive motions practice."

Jacobsen didn't seem to be grinning any more. "Have it your way, Mr. Brunelle. May the best lawyer win."

Brunelle loved getting an opening like that. He hoped Jacobsen would be as sloppy in front of the jury. "No, Mr. Jacobsen. May justice win."

CHAPTER 12

The motions kept coming. By the day of the bail hearing, Brunelle had been served with the Motion to Change Conditions of Release, plus a Motion to Change Venue, a Motion to Compel Discovery, a Motion to Dismiss for Insufficient Evidence, and a Motion for Leave to File More Motions. Actually, the last one was just something Brunelle thought of cynically as the pleadings piled up, but unfortunately, Jacobsen didn't need permission to file more motions. He could file as many as he wanted, frivolous or not, and Brunelle would just have to respond to each and every one of them. In civil cases, frivolous motions were subject to monetary sanctions against client and counsel. In criminal cases, they were lauded as zealous advocacy in defense of the accused.

Brunelle checked his mailbox on the way down to court. No new motions as of 8:53 a.m. The courtroom was packed, but then again it usually was that time of day. The bail hearing had to be scheduled in front of the judge who had originally set bail, and the judge who had originally set bail was the one who was assigned to the arraignment/plea court that six-month rotation. Judge Gary Douglas, who took pleas all morning and did arraignments all afternoon. So going back in front of him meant scheduling the bail hearing right before a morning docket full of guilty pleas. So the courtroom was full, but not necessarily for the sex club case. It was just full of criminals and their friends and families.

The one news camera was there for Brunelle though. Or more correctly, it was there for Master Michael Atkins and his attorney *du jour*, Ron Jacobsen. Brunelle was just window dressing. But that was no reason not to say 'Hi' to the cameraman and reporter.

"Hey, Jack. Hey, Bill," he greeted them as he passed through the gallery toward the secure courtroom behind the bulletproof glass.

"Hey, Dave," Bill, the reporter, replied. "Any chance we can get a sound bite from you after the hearing?"

Brunelle smiled. "Depends on the ruling," he quipped. But really, it didn't. He was going to stay far away from the cameras on this one. There was no way he could discuss the details without being at least R-rated. Accordingly, anything he said could potentially be inflammatory, and therefore unethical. The last thing he needed was the Bar Association up his ass while he tried to get his conviction.

He stepped through the door and found Jacobsen and Master Michael already waiting for him, seated comfortably at one of the two counsel tables within. Jacobsen was a big guy. Easily 6'3" and well over two hundred pounds. He was in his fifties and was at that stage just before he started to look exhausted from having carried that large frame around his whole life.

The only person missing was Yamata. She had other cases of course and had another hearing scheduled at the same time Jacobsen had set the bail hearing. Rather than try to get Jacobsen to agree to reschedule—the definition of 'quixotic'...which Brunelle had had to look up after Yamata used the word—they figured

Brunelle could probably handle a simple bail hearing by himself.

Brunelle preferred to stand at the bar in that particular courtroom, so he set his file on the counter and greeted the young prosecutor whose unfortunate assignment was to do pleas all morning, every morning. The only break came in the afternoon, when that same prosecutor would do arraignments all afternoon, every afternoon.

"Morning, Jason," he said. "Can I go first?"

The young attorney nodded a bit too emphatically. "Oh, of course, Mr. Brunelle."

Brunelle smiled slightly and sighed. He'd been around long enough for the young attorneys to mean it when they used the title 'Mister.' But there was another young attorney in the courtroom who he didn't mind when she used the word 'Mister.'

"Hiya, Mr. B." Robyn waved to him from her spot leaning alluringly against the far wall. She was with the public defender's office and as a junior attorney there, she'd be spending her day handling the other side of the assembly line of pleas and arraignments.

Brunelle, the professional orator, felt that usual moment of speechlessness whenever he saw the young redhead, but he was saved by the sudden entry of Judge Douglas.

"All rise!" commanded the bailiff. Brunelle was already standing, but Jacobsen, Atkins, and the gallery all complied. After a moment, Judge Douglas sat down on the bench and informed the courtroom, "You may be seated."

Then he looked to Brunelle and Jacobsen. "Are the parties ready on the matter of State versus Atkins?"

Both attorneys replied in the affirmative, and Judge Douglas wasted no time taking control of the hearing. He was in his late fifties, about average age for a Superior Court judge, and had been doing the job long enough to know how to respect the attorneys without letting them take over.

"I'll hear first from Mr. Jacobsen," he announced.

Jacobsen rose importantly. "Thank you, Your Honor. I have brought this motion on behalf of Mr. Atkins to ask the court to modify his conditions of release. We are requesting two things. First, we would ask you to exonerate Mr. Atkins' bail and release him on his own recognizance. He has no prior criminal history and has gone to the trouble and expense of hiring an attorney. Indeed, I am the second attorney on this case. Mr. Atkins takes this matter so seriously that he dismissed his prior attorney, after paying him far more money than that attorney's experience might have warranted, and then hired my firm, again at no small expense. Mr. Atkins is more than adequately invested financially in this case. There is no reason to hold even more of his money in the clerk's office."

And Brunelle then realized how Atkins could afford a new lawyer: he was counting on getting his bail money back.

"In addition," Jacobsen continued, "the court previously ordered that my client have no contact with the establishment where this unfortunate event occurred. We are asking the court to lift that restriction. This case was not a homicide, it was an accident. There is no risk that Mr. Atkins might injure anyone else at the club. Moreover, the club has long since reopened for business, so the crime scene has been more than corrupted. There is no danger that allowing Mr. Atkins to reconnect with his support community will result in evidence being compromised. Accordingly, in addition to exonerating bail, the court should also lift that particular restriction. Thank you, Your Honor. I stand ready, should the court have any questions."

Judge Douglas didn't have any. He turned to Brunelle. "The State's response?"

This was the tricky part. Jacobsen had a point. Actually, he had two points. And they were good points. Atkins wasn't going to flee the jurisdiction and he was probably not going to choke out another sex partner. And he was already out, having posted the bail. There was no good reason to keep the money. On top of that, the crime scene was undoubtedly corrupted. Again and again, most likely. It was the only time Brunelle ever hoped a crime scene was cleaned with bleach. There wasn't a great reason to keep Atkins out of his bondage barn. But it was standard operating procedure: homicide defendants have high bail, and all defendants have to stay away from the crime scene.

Brunelle valued his credibility more than inconveniencing Atkins. He could go histrionic and implore the court to deny these outrageous requests. But he was going to be appearing in front of Douglas for years and years to come, long after Master Michael had been tried, convicted, and served his sentence.

On the other hand, he didn't have to roll over either.

"Thank you, Your Honor," he began. "The State would ask the court to deny both requests. I'll decline to respond to Mr. Jacobsen's characterization of the crime as merely an accident. A bail hearing isn't the place to litigate the merits of the case. The questions for the court are whether the defendant is a flight risk or a danger to the community. I would simply say that as long as the court has kept Mr. Atkins' bail money he has appeared for court. I see no reason to change that situation. As far as his request to return to the crime scene, I find it curious that he would claim that he has lost the love of his life, but at the same time he's eager to get back to the, uh, establishment where he can apparently find a replacement. The court should follow its usual procedure and exclude the defendant from the crime scene. I'm sure there are other similar clubs where he can pursue his... interests."

Brunelle intended for the last remark to be snarky. If he wasn't going to win the hearing, he could at least poke the defendant a bit. And besides, it helped cover his own budding interests in the area.

Douglas nodded and looked back to Jacobsen. "It's your motion, Mr. Jacobsen. You have the last word."

Jacobsen stood up again to address the judge. "Thank you, Your Honor. I would disagree with Brunelle that a bail hearing is no place to discuss the facts of the case. The facts are vital for the court to make a bail decision. A young woman is dead. If she had been premeditatively murdered by Mr. Atkins, perhaps during a robbery or other crime, and Mr. Atkins had then fled to another state and had to be extradited to face charges, those would all be reasons for a high bail. But here, we have a terrible, tragic accident. Unfortunately, accidents happen. My client did lose the love of his life, despite Mr. Brunelle's callous comments. He remained at the scene to speak with the authorities and has appeared for every court date he has had. He is not a flight risk and he is not a danger to anyone. The court should grant our motions. Thank you."

Douglas took just a moment to chew his cheek. There was an entire docket of pleas waiting, so he wasn't about to waste time.

"I agree with Mr. Jacobsen. The court rules require the court to presume a personal recognizance release in all but capital cases. This is not a capital case. Mr. Atkins has appeared for court and hired private counsel. I will exonerate bail and release Mr. Atkins on his own recognizance."

Brunelle nodded slightly. Douglas had been in private practice before ascending to the bench. He understood how important it was for a lawyer to get paid.

"In addition, I can see no further reason to exclude Mr. Atkins from..." he looked down at the charging documents and raised an eyebrow, "the Cu-CUM-ber Club. That particular restriction will be lifted."

Brunelle nodded again. He's lost the motions, but they were good motions to lose. Atkins was already out and who really cared if he went and fucked someone else at that sex club? Brunelle cared a lot more about the more important motions that were coming down the pike.

"Thank you, Your Honor," Brunelle said. "I'll prepare a new order."

The conditions of release orders were preprinted, fill-in-the-blank forms that were kept in a pocket on the wall next to other standard arraignment and plea forms. In a few moments, Brunelle had filled in the proper blanks and handed the form up to Judge Douglas. After Douglas signed it, Jacobsen took his copies and left with a very happy client.

Brunelle started to leave too, but as he passed, Robyn stepped off the wall and grabbed his arm. "Please tell me you're keeping your powder dry," she whispered.

Brunelle's brow furrowed. "What do you mean?" He mimicked her hushed tone as the judge went ahead with the rest of the docket.

"That other lawyer—" Robyn began.

"Jacobsen."

"Right. He kicked your ass with that whole 'accidents happen' bullshit. You didn't respond at all."

"It's not relevant," Brunelle insisted. "You don't litigate the merits of the case at a bail hearing. It's about safety of the community and risk of flight."

Robyn cocked her head at him. "Seriously? I mean, sure, technically, that's true, but really, we always argue the merits. The judge isn't gonna hold someone who might actually be innocent."

Brunelle knew that was probably true, but he didn't see why it mattered. "Honestly, I don't really care. He's already out and is he wants to go back to the Cu-CUM-ber club, what do I care? Maybe he'll kill someone else and I can add charges."

Robyn just stared at him. He felt her gaze sizing him up,

trying to figure out if he was as dense as he was apparently coming off.

"There's a way to win this case," she finally said.

Brunelle nodded. "Okay," he encouraged. But she didn't elaborate.

"I mean, I don't want you to win or anything," she quickly corrected. "Not professionally. We're on opposite sides. But personally... Well, like I said, there's a way to win this case, but you don't seem to get it."

Brunelle frowned. Despite his dismissive attitude, he knew she was right. And he knew he needed to figure it out. "So educate me."

Unexpressed thoughts flashed behind Robyn's eyes. "You know I want to."

Brunelle nodded. He wanted that too. Way more than he should. He was smart enough to walk away before it was too late. "Thanks anyway, Robyn. I guess I'll try to figure it out by myself."

Robyn's expression hardened back to her usual smiling mask. But she didn't manage to say anything as he extracted his arm from her welcome grip and walked out of the courtroom.

When Brunelle got back to the office, he stopped by his legal assistant's desk. He needed to get his thoughts back on the case. "Did Jacobsen file any more motions while we were in court?" he joked.

Nicole offered a pained grin. "Actually, yes." She picked up two different documents and handed the top one to Brunelle.

He read the caption. "Motion to Dismiss for Prosecutorial Misconduct? What misconduct?"

"I'm guessing it's the same as this." She handed him the other document.

Brunelle's heart sank as he looked down at the letterhead of the Washington State Bar Association.

Dear Mr. Brunelle,

This letter is to inform you that a bar complaint has been filed against you...

CHAPTER 13

Brunelle stormed into the examining room at the King County Medical Examiner's office.

"A bar complaint!" he shouted. "I got a fucking bar complaint!"

Kat Anderson looked up from where she had been about to start the Y-incision to open the next cadaver on the day's autopsy list. "Good for you. I've got a dead body. Wanna trade?"

Brunelle crossed his arms. "Hardee-har-har. This is serious."

Kat raised an eyebrow and set down her scalpel. She crossed her own arms. "Did you just 'hardee-har-har' me? Really?"

Brunelle waved her remark away. "Look, this is a big deal. I wanted to talk to you about this, but when I called you didn't answer."

"When you called," Kat replied, arms still crossed, "I was doing my job."

"You can't take a minute when your boyfriend wants to talk?"

Kat surrendered a tight smile. "Boyfriend? Okay, that I can handle. You never say that."

Brunelle smiled. "Yeah, well… You're welcome."

Kat shook her head amicably. "I wasn't thanking you for accurately describing our relationship. Just amused by you actually admitting it. But really, sometimes you can be such a girl."

Brunelle dropped his arms. "A girl? What the hell does that mean?"

Kat laughed. "It means, Mr. Boyfriend," she stepped forward and tousled his hair with a latex-gloved hand, "that sometimes you just want to share your feelings. It's cute. Inconvenient sometimes, usually irritating, but cute."

Brunelle frowned. "I like being cute to you, but I'm thinking maybe not this way."

"No worries, handsome." Kat picked up her scalpel again. "I usually just let you talk 'til you're done. But really, I have work to do."

"Yeah, but I got a bar complaint," Brunelle repeated. "That seriously sucks."

"So do I," Kat purred, "but not if you keep up this whining. I would think this is an occupational hazard. Who filed it?"

Brunelle's brain was torn between responding to the question she ended with, or the sexual allusion she started with. Primacy versus recency. He opted for the question. "Uh, that defendant. Atkins. Master Michael." Then, after a moment's thought, he added, "Fucker."

"Right," Kat laughed. "As I recall, that's exactly what he was doing when he choked her out. But why did he file a bar complaint? What did you do?"

"I didn't do anything!" Brunelle threw his hands up. "I fucking met with him. With his attorney present. At his request."

Kat cocked her head. "How does that equal a bar complaint?"

Brunelle shrugged. "Prosecutors aren't allowed to talk with defendants directly. Not unless they're representing themselves.

Otherwise we have to go through their lawyers."

"Then why did you meet with him?" Kat questioned. "Didn't you know better?"

"No, it's okay if you do it with their lawyer present," Brunelle explained. "I don't like doing it. It rarely helps. But Lannigan insisted. He thought I could talk him into pleading guilty."

Kat's brows knitted together. "His lawyer wanted you to talk his client into pleading guilty? No wonder he filed a bar complaint."

"His lawyer," Brunelle corrected indignantly, "invited me to explain the strength of the State's case to his client. I obliged. I didn't do anything wrong."

"You talked directly to a murder defendant."

"He's a manslaughter defendant," Brunelle replied. "And his lawyer was present."

"Still," Kat said, "you probably should have said no. There's a reason you don't usually do it."

Brunelle frowned. He knew she was right. But that didn't mean he deserved a bar complaint. "I didn't break the rules."

Kat smiled and stepped back, looking Brunelle up and down once. "Well, maybe that's your problem, Mr. Brunelle. Always following the rules, instead of doing what your gut tells you. Must be the prosecutor in you."

Brunelle felt a bit stung. He'd come for support and understanding, not rebuke and pop psychology. But he didn't want a fight. Not right then. And not with Kat. "Sure. That's probably it."

Kat tipped her head toward the cadaver on her examining table. "Look, I really do have to get back to work. Sorry you got a bar complaint. Really. But maybe it's a good thing. Next time you get invited to do something, instead of following the rules, just do what your gut tells you."

Brunelle nodded. "Sure," he repeated. Then he straightened up again. "Okay, well, I guess I'll head out. Thanks for the advice."

But as he walked out, he couldn't help but think she shouldn't have said what she said. When he got outside and checked his phone for messages, he was sure of it.

He had two new texts. Both from Robyn.

'OK. I'll help you. You need it.'

Then, *'You know you want to.'*

And damn if he didn't.

CHAPTER 14

Brunelle actually summoned the self-control not to respond to Robyn's text immediately. Even that night, while Kat was busy with Lizzy and other non-him stuff, he still managed not to answer her. But he read the texts again and again and let his mind wander into places it ought not to have.

By the next morning he was glad to have work to distract him. Until work reminded him there were a lot more serious things to deal with than a cute defense attorney.

"There's a Peter Sylvan here to see you," the receptionist told him over the phone.

Sylvan? Brunelle paused, trying to place the name. But he couldn't. He didn't know any defense attorneys with that name and he didn't recall any victim families with the last name 'Sylvan.'

"Did he say what case it's on?"

"No, Mr. Brunelle," the receptionist answered. "I asked, but he said it was better if he didn't say."

Fuck, Brunelle thought. He looked over at his in-box. Still sitting on top was the letter from the Bar Association. They'd sent an investigator already. He wasn't ready for that.

"Uh," he stammered into the phone. "Tell him I'll be out in a minute." Then he thought twice. "I'll be right there," he corrected.

"Tell him I'll be right there."

You don't keep the bar investigator waiting.

Brunelle stood up and looked around his office. Professionally tidy. All the files in the file cabinet, the in-box not too full, and the computer open to the word processor, not the internet.

Good. First impressions were important.

He checked his tie in the mirror behind his door then walked out to the lobby. With a little luck, maybe the investigator was just there as a formality before dismissing the complaint. Maybe he'd already talked to Lannigan. Lannigan would back him up, right?

Brunelle shook the thought from his head. It didn't matter if Lannigan backed him up. He hadn't done anything wrong. He'd followed the rules. It was important to follow the rules.

He stepped into the small reception area and extended a hand. "Peter?" Brunelle chose the friendliness of a first name greeting over the formality of a 'Mr. Sylvan.' They were colleagues, not enemies—he hoped "It's a pleasure to meet you."

Sylvan turned around from where he'd been scrutinizing one of the framed prints on the lobby wall. A photo of some loggers from turn-of-the-century Seattle. He looked to be a bit younger than Brunelle, and stood a bit taller as well, with long brown hair pulled back into a tidy ponytail, and an expensive-looking suit under an even more expensive looking overcoat.

Nice to know my bar dues are paying this guy's obviously exorbitant salary, Brunelle thought. But he kept his smile pasted on.

"Mr. Brunelle," Sylvan reached out and seized Brunelle's hand in a strong, warm grasp. "I'm sorry to drop in unannounced. I find it easier sometimes, given the nature of my work."

Brunelle nodded a little too much. "Oh, of course. Understood. Why don't we go back to my office?"

Sylvan released his hand. "Good idea. Then we can talk candidly."

Candidly, Brunelle thought ruefully. Sometimes he hated that word. Wasn't it enough just to be honest? Did he have to be candid too? "Sounds good," he said anyway.

They walked the short distance to Brunelle's office. Brunelle noticed a few of the legal secretaries eying Sylvan as they passed. Brunelle had to concede, Sylvan was an attractive enough man. Apparently, it wasn't enough just to have Brunelle's entire professional future in his hands—he had to look good doing it.

Once inside the office, Brunelle sat at his desk. Sylvan took the liberty of closing the door and sat in one of the guest chairs. Brunelle frowned slightly at the door-closing. It was generally a better idea not to have a conversation without witnesses. On the other hand, maybe he didn't need everyone in the office talking about his bar complaint. He decided to just jump right in.

"I want you to know," he started, raising his hand for emphasis, "that I'm fully aware of the rules for this sort of thing."

Sylvan raised an eyebrow. "Oh really?"

Brunelle nodded. "Yes. Absolutely. I take this sort of thing very seriously. I've been practicing for a long time now and I know what I can and can't do."

Sylvan leaned forward and pressed his fingertips together. "Well, I'm glad to hear that. One never knows what other people might know about this sort of thing."

Brunelle could sense a tone of approval in Sylvan's voice. That was a relief. Maybe this would go well after all. "Well, I think if you're going to do something, you should do it well. I care a lot about the quality of my work."

"I see," Sylvan replied, nodding. "And how long have you been--how did you phrase it?--practicing?"

Brunelle cocked his head slightly. *Why wouldn't I say 'practicing'? That's what you do. You practice law.* But he let the comment go. "Almost nineteen years."

Both of Sylvan's eyebrows shot up this time. Brunelle didn't know why that would have surprised him. He could have looked up when Brunelle was first admitted to the bar. "I daresay, Mr. Brunelle," Sylvan said, "if you've been doing this sort of thing for nineteen years, you're no longer just practicing. You're a Master."

Brunelle shrugged and tried not to blush. "Yes, well..."

"Unless, that is," Sylvan interrupted with a polite laugh, "you're a submissive. I shouldn't assume. Either way, after nineteen years, you're obviously aware of the subtle contours of the dominant-submissive relationship."

Brunelle's jaw dropped open and he blinked several times at his guest.

"Actually," Sylvan went on, "I'm a bit surprised. Mr. Jacobsen didn't mention you had experience in this area. But then again, maybe he didn't know. People tend to tell me things they don't tell others."

Brunelle sat motionless for several more seconds, then nodded slowly, realizing the mistake he'd made. "You're not from the bar association, are you?"

It was Sylvan's turn to cock his head. "The bar association?" he asked. Then he let out a deep laugh. "No, Mr. Brunelle. I'm not from your licensing agency. But that does explain your responses. I was rather surprised—and impressed. But no, I'm not from the bar. I'm a sexologist. I specialize in nonreciprocal power relationships coupled with device and restraint protocols."

Brunelle blinked again, his mind caught between the embarrassing mistake he'd made and his efforts to understand what Sylvan had just said.

"Bondage," Sylvan translated. "That's what it's simplistically called by people who don't really understand it." He paused, then added, "And I'm thinking you fall into that category after all, eh, Mr. Brunelle?"

Brunelle felt the blush coming again. He was about to protest that he and his girlfriend had played a little bit, thank you very much, but some sense of 'kiss and tell' propriety made him hesitate just long enough.

"And don't tell me you've played around with silk ribbons and holding hands over heads," Sylvan repeated. "I'm talking about something far more complex, far more sophisticated than that sort of vanilla experimentation. In fact, that's what I like to call 'French vanilla.' It may claim to have a touch more flavor, but when all is said and done, it's still just vanilla."

Brunelle's mind stopped racing between thoughts of Kat, his neckties, and Robyn, just long enough to think rationally for a moment. If this wasn't the bar investigator—and it certainly wasn't—then...

"Why are you here?" Brunelle demanded, a bit testily at that point. He didn't need his sexuality diminished by some ponytailed sexologist off the street. "Just professional interest in one of my cases?"

Sylvan took a moment, then leaned back in his seat again. "I'm afraid not, Mr. Brunelle. I believe I mentioned Mr. Jacobsen, the lawyer for Mr. Atkins?"

Brunelle nodded. He did recall that amid the embarrassing misunderstanding and subsequent belittlement.

"I've been retained by Mr. Jacobsen as an expert in the field of atypical sexual activities," Sylvan explained. "If you don't understand the relationship between Michael and Tina—and it's clear you don't—then the jury is likely to misunderstand it as well. It will be my job to educate them."

Great, Brunelle thought. *That should be... awkward.*

"In any event," Sylvan continued, "I wanted to introduce myself. I was in the courthouse anyway on an unrelated matter, so I thought I'd stop by. This sort of thing is usually better discussed in person than over the phone anyway. I thought Mr. Jacobsen had sent you an email with my resume, but apparently not. I'll remind him to do that when we meet to discuss my testimony."

Sylvan stood up.

"I must say," he admitted, "I'm a bit disappointed that whole nineteen years thing was a misunderstanding. I was looking forward to being cross-examined by someone who actually knew what they were talking about. Oh well."

He extended a hand to Brunelle, who shook it despite everything. He was just relieved the encounter was ending. "Thanks for stopping by, Mr. Sylvan," he said.

"Doctor," Sylvan corrected. "Dr. Sylvan. I have a Ph.D. in sexology."

Brunelle managed a tight smile. "Of course you do."

He walked Sylvan back to the lobby, then returned to his desk and checked his spam filter. Sure enough, there was an email from Jacobsen from two days earlier, with Sylvan's resume attached. Brunelle didn't click on it. He knew enough.

He knew enough to know he didn't know enough.

He pulled out his phone and finally sent his reply to Robyn: *OK I'll let you help me.*

Then he decided to be honest: *I need your help.*

And finally, he decided to be candid: *I need you.*

CHAPTER 15

"It's nice to be needed," Robyn remarked as they sat down at the small table in the corner of the restaurant.

It was one of the nicest places Brunelle had ever been to, even if it was uncomfortably close to The Jade House where he and Kat regularly ate. It was called simply 'The Pond' and was hidden in the back of an unevenly paved parking lot, behind a strip mall of Asian markets at the edge of Seattle's International District. He'd driven past that particular group of shops more times than he could count, but he'd never noticed the restaurant tucked away in the back. It was the kind of place he would have taken Kat to impress her and try get some action that night. Instead, Robyn had chosen it. He was pretty sure he knew what that meant.

The food was Vietnamese, the décor impeccable, and the lighting a perfect level of romantic dim. The *maître d'* had taken one look at the old man with the young beauty and seated them in the back corner, partially behind some potted palms. More than enough privacy to discuss whatever such a couple might want to discuss over a late dinner.

Brunelle shook his head as he sat down. *If they only knew.*

"Uh, yeah," he fumbled his reply. "I guess I need your help

after all."

Brunelle wasn't bad with women. He knew how to play the game. He knew switching back from needing Robyn to just needing her help wasn't going to go unnoticed. But it was hard to play the game when he expected his quarterback to walk in any minute and find him giving the playbook to another team. Despite the splendor of The Pond, he was starting to wish they'd maybe gone someplace else.

Like Portland.

On the other hand, it was walking distance to Robyn's apartment, and he'd parked his car there, so no matter how things went, he was walking her back to her building. Maybe they could just grab an appetizer and leave before the QB showed up.

Robyn frowned at his reply, but her eyes held the smile still. "Oh, my *help*. Right." She looked around the romantic restaurant. "Strictly business then. Well, at least I can write it off on my taxes."

Brunelle grimaced. If he wasn't careful he could end up pissing off both women. So he did what he was best at: spinning with words, suggesting without saying, tempting without promising.

"Just because I said I need your help," he answered, "doesn't mean that's all I need."

The smile returned to Robyn's lips, made that much more seductive in the half-light. "Smooth, Mr. Brunelle," she acknowledged. "But remember: I know what we do for a living. I do it too. We twist words to get what we want."

Brunelle crossed his arms but maintained his own careful grin. "Maybe you do that, but I'm a prosecutor. My job is to seek the truth."

Robyn didn't say anything for a long moment. Then she burst out laughing. "Oh, fuck you, Dave." She shook her beautiful head, the red curls bouncing. "Didn't you learn anything playing defense attorney down in Cali?"

That stung. Not the accusation that he'd been too stubborn to learn from his brief experience as a defense attorney. And not being reminded about Kat, the one who'd convinced him to go to California in the first place; Kat wasn't a sting—she was a dull ache in the back of his heart. No, what stung was that laugh. He didn't like being laughed at. He didn't like Robyn laughing at him.

It broke the trance. He suddenly realized he was an older man with a younger woman hiding in the corner of a romantic restaurant, pretending to be there to talk shop, but really thinking about, hoping for, but also afraid of what might happen between them after dinner. He shook his own head slightly, at himself. "Right," he agreed weakly. "Good point. I was just kidding. But, uh, you know, this case is more difficult than I thought. You said you might have some insights?"

The waiter arrived before Robyn could answer. A young Asian man, dressed sharply in all black. He gave them each a glass of water with lemon, plus a pot of tea and a promise to return in a few minutes to take their orders.

Robyn rested her pretty face on her hand and scrutinized Brunelle across the table. Brunelle felt the weight of her stare and was glad the restaurant was dark enough that the burning in his cheeks was likely unapparent. He let his own gaze caress her features. She really was beautiful. Stunning even. That one dimple was clearly visible as she grinned at him. Brunelle's eyes drifted to the other cheek where the scar was only partially hidden by the dimness. He couldn't imagine how anyone else could wear a facial scar with such magnificence. It wasn't a scar; it was a beauty mark.

He was so caught up in the radiance of her face that he was actually startled when she finally spoke, doubly so by her words.

"I know you're fucking the medical examiner," she said. "I kinda don't care."

Brunelle felt his heart break into a sprint even as any potential response got stuck in his throat. Still, something inside him made him feel the need to defend his relationship with Kat. "I'm not just fucking her..." he started, but he lost where he might go next.

Robyn smirked. "Oh, right. She's your girlfriend."

Brunelle still chafed a bit at the whole 'boyfriend-girlfriend' label. He wasn't sure why. It just seemed so high school. Nevertheless, he went ahead and adopted it. "Yeah." But not with much conviction.

"She's just your girlfriend, right?" Robyn pressed. "Not fiancée? Not wife?"

Brunelle shook his head. "No, just my—" but he choked on the 'girlfriend' word that time. "We date, I guess."

"You mean you fuck," Robyn laughed. "A couple times a week, right? Maybe dinner beforehand?"

Brunelle shrugged. It was more than that.

"Kinda like you and I are doing right now?" Robyn tested.

Brunelle shifted in his seat. He didn't like being so transparent. "I thought we we're talking about my case."

Robyn lowered her eyes at him. "Really, Dave? You could have called me. We could have met in the Pit. Shit, we could have grabbed a coffee from the stand in the courthouse lobby. But none of those are gonna get you down my pants, are they?"

Brunelle wasn't sure what to say. So Robyn kept talking.

"So, what's the deal, Dave? Do you and Dr. Dead have rules about this?"

Brunelle cocked his head. "Rules?"

"Yeah, rules," Robyn confirmed. "Can you see other people? You're not married, right? Shit, a lot of marriages are open, but they have rules, ya know? Each partner knows what the rules are. What are your rules with Kitty Kat?"

Brunelle thought about it for a second. He and Kat had never discussed whether they could see other people. It never came up. He knew why, though. Of course they couldn't see other people. That's what it meant to be boyfriend-girlfriend. ...Didn't it?

"Uh," Brunelle stammered, "we don't really have rules. I mean, we haven't talked about it."

Robyn shook her head at him. "Tsk, tsk, sir. You have to have rules. How can you be safe if you don't know the rules?"

Brunelle wasn't sure. "I don't know."

Robyn reached across the table and patted his hand. It was more motherly than sexual, but the feel of her flesh on his aroused him anyway. "I know. That's your problem. You're a rule-follower but you don't even know the rules."

Brunelle turned his hand over and grasped hers. His grip was strong. He could tell she liked it. "So where's the rule book?"

Robyn tugged slightly on her hand, but only to see if he'd let go. He didn't. She smiled and met his gaze under lidded eyes. "It's at my apartment."

CHAPTER 16

Despite the urge to leave for Robyn's apartment right then, they actually stayed for dinner. Brunelle was glad for two reasons. First, the food was excellent. Cashew chicken, five stars. Second, it gave his blood time to cool--and redirect itself upwards to his brain. By the time they reached Robyn's apartment, Brunelle had managed to recover whatever part of him remembered the rule about staying faithful to his girlfriend.

Robyn stepped up onto the small porch at the entrance of her apartment building. When Brunelle didn't follow, she turned back. "Aren't you coming up?"

Brunelle took a deep breath. There had been few things in his life he'd wanted to do more than he wanted to do Robyn right then. But somehow he managed to say, "I think maybe I shouldn't."

One thing Brunelle had first noticed about Robyn was how she always seemed to be smiling. Even those times her mouth traded the grin for a more serious expression, the spark of her smile still twinkled in her eyes. So he was struck not so much by his sudden flash of will power in refusing her as by the stony expression it elicited.

She stared at him for several long seconds, through

narrowed, smile-less eyes. Finally, she shoved a fist onto a perfectly curved hip and said, "Are you fucking kidding me?"

Brunelle shrugged and looked down. He didn't like her eyes without the smile. "I think it's probably better if we say goodnight out here."

He looked back up to see her still staring at him, her disbelief fully apparent on those perfect features of hers. After a moment, she cracked a grin, then glanced down and shook her head. When she looked up again, the smile-light had returned to her eyes. She stepped off the porch and right into Brunelle's space. He didn't step away and she laid a hand on his chest, then looked up into his eyes.

Brunelle's heart almost beat out of his chest. If she'd ordered him inside right then, he would have obeyed. He would have done anything she'd asked. But she didn't ask him anything. Instead, she told him something.

"*You* texted me. *You* said you needed me. *You* asked me out to dinner. I picked the place, but you paid. And you walked me all the way home. *You* did all that. Not me, you." She took his chin in her hand. Her grip was hot and strong. "But now you're telling me no."

She looked down and shook her head. "That hurts my feelings."

Then she shoved him away by his face and leveled a glare that bore right through him. "And that's against the rules."

CHAPTER 17

The next morning was painful. In part because of the regret of not having spent the night with Robyn. In part because of the hangover from trying to drown that regret in whiskey when he got home. But mostly because, this time, the unexpected visitor at the front window really was an investigator from the bar association.

At least she's pretty, Brunelle thought. Tall, thin, long black curls, and fashionable glasses. He could think of worse things to look at as he watched his career slip away from him.

Brunelle smiled as he extended his hand in greeting. "Dave Brunelle."

The investigator shook it with a warm, firm grasp. "Yvonne Taylor, from the Bar Association. Nice to meet you. Do you have a few minutes to speak with me this morning?"

Brunelle knew the right answer. "Of course. I always have time for the Bar Association."

Some of his defense attorney friends had a saying: 'Bar card first.' It meant clients—especially criminal defendants—were likely to ask you to do things which were morally questionable and professionally unethical. Even if the requests were tempting in their potential effectiveness, it wouldn't do anyone any good if you lost your bar license. No single defendant was worth that. It didn't come up nearly as often for prosecutors. Victims usually didn't ask you to do unethical things; cops weren't supposed to. Either way it was easy to say no.

Unless, Brunelle realized, it was a defense attorney asking you to do something that wasn't actually unethical but the criminal defendant would file a bar complaint anyway.

Brunelle led her back to his office and they took their respective stances. Taylor, sitting in a guest chair, the predator. Brunelle, the prey, hiding behind his desk.

"I'll try to make this quick," she said. "You've received our letter. It outlines the allegations against you. Primarily, the grievant is alleging that you violated Rule of Professional Conduct 4.2, which prohibits a lawyer from directly contacting a person he knows is represented by an attorney."

"Well, see," Brunelle tried to smile casually, "his lawyer was the one who asked me to talk with him and he was present the entire time."

Taylor just stared at him for a moment. She was frozen in the conversational pose she'd been in as she'd finished her last sentence. She looked like a statue of a pretty bar investigator. She waited long enough to make it uncomfortable, then said, "I wasn't finished."

Brunelle's heart sank. It already wasn't going well. He became acutely aware that his future was in the hands of a stranger who may not have the background and experience to truly understand who he was or what he did. And then he realized that was probably how Master Michael felt about him.

He leaned back and sat up straight in his desk chair. "I'm sorry. Please. Go ahead."

Taylor waited another long moment. The kind of long moment designed to make sure the other party knows who's in control. Brunelle knew. He didn't like it, but he knew. Then she spoke again.

"As I was saying," she drew the words out, "it is a violation of the Rules of Professional Conduct for a lawyer to directly contact someone the lawyer knows is represented by counsel. Such communication must go through the represented person's counsel. That is the allegation against you. My job is to investigate the circumstances to determine whether the RPCs have been violated. If so, it will be up to the Discipline Committee to determine what sanction to impose." Another pause. Brunelle knew not to interrupt. He also guessed what she was going to say next. "Up to and including disbarment."

Brunelle knew that was a mostly empty threat. Even if they decided he shouldn't have talked with Master Michael, it was unlikely they would pull his license. He'd probably just get an admonishment. Or maybe a formal reprimand. Probably not an actual suspension. And almost certainly not disbarment.

Then again, he couldn't believe he was in trouble with the bar in the first place. It was just a misunderstanding. An accident.

"Do you even know the actual language of RPC 4.2?" Taylor challenged.

Brunelle frowned slightly. He glanced at the book of court rules on his bookshelf. "Not off the top of my head," he admitted.

Taylor crossed her arms and shook her head. "How can you know whether you've violated a rule if you don't even know the rules?"

Brunelle nodded. "That's a good point." He thought for a moment, although not really about the bar complaint. "What's the best way to learn the rules?"

Taylor nodded toward the same set of court rules. "Go straight to the source. And don't just read the rule you think you might be violating. Read them all. You can't understand a single rule unless you understand how they all interrelate."

Brunelle nodded again. That made a lot of sense. A lot.

Taylor leaned forward. "Look, Mr. Brunelle. I don't need to tell you, this is a big deal. Allegedly infringing on a criminal defendant's right to counsel is something we take very seriously. This could very well impact your ability to practice. Have you considering hiring an attorney with experience in this field?"

"Experience?" Brunelle asked. "Are there attorneys who specialize in defending against bar complaints?"

Taylor nodded. "Yes. Just a few, but they know what they're doing. It's a specialized practice. Most of them are former bar investigators like me."

Brunelle grinned darkly. "Something to fall back on later?" he suggested.

Taylor cracked a smile. "Maybe. But for now, I'm after you. So you better get some help."

Brunelle took the threat for what it was: professional only. "What's my other choice?" he asked

Taylor shrugged. "Maybe you have a colleague who has experience with this sort of thing. I suppose you could ask their advice. But if you defend yourself, you'll have to do all the research on your own and hope you get it right. Serious research, too," she warned, "not playing around at the edges and making it up as you go along." She leaned forward, her black curls falling over her shoulder. "But really, Mr. Brunelle, I don't advise that."

Brunelle pursed his lips and tapped them with a thoughtful finger. He considered his options. He'd recently met an expert in the field. He knew a colleague who was more experienced. But he knew, deep down, he was a loner. He liked to do things himself. Maybe that was the problem.

A smile appeared on Brunelle's features despite the circumstances. "Thank you, Ms. Taylor," he replied, again not really to the topic at hand. "But I kind of like doing my own research."

CHAPTER 18

He couldn't go back to the Cu-CUM-ber Club. That would be too obvious. People might recognize him. Luckily it was Seattle. And Capitol Hill. There were more sex clubs up there than Starbucks, and that was saying something.

And he couldn't bring his research partner. He probably should have, but somehow he couldn't. Or he didn't want to. He needed to be himself, not Kat's boyfriend.

And he couldn't really be himself. Not Dave Brunelle. He wasn't famous, but he didn't need his name remembered later if anyone started asking questions. So he decided he'd be 'Andrew Brown.' 'Andrew' because that was his middle name. 'Brown' because 'Brunelle' was French for brunette. So in a way, it was still his name; just not in a way anyone would recognize it.

"Welcome, Andrew," said the shapely woman at the front door of The Opal Room. He paid his cover and she opened the door to the club. "I hope you enjoy yourself."

Brunelle nodded. He was sure he would.

That was part of the problem.

Inside was dark. That was the first thing he noticed. But maybe not as dark as he would have liked. He would have preferred sufficient dimness to feel anonymous. Instead, it was dim enough to be comfortable but bright enough that he would definitely be recognized if he ran into someone he knew.

But he didn't really expect that. Matt Duncan wasn't going to be caught dead anywhere near there. Kat was home with Lizzy — he'd confirmed that before deciding what night to go. And Robyn.... Well, she was a regular at the Cu-CUM-ber Club, right?

Somehow, that last thought actually made him a little angry. Angry at her that she would be with someone else, even though he turned her down. And angry at himself for turning her down. And just angry at the whole situation. Robyn should have been there with him, playing tour guide. Kat probably would have come if he'd asked her. But he didn't ask her.

Damn, he wished it were darker in there.

Surveying the main room, it didn't look that much different from any other bar or nightclub he'd been in. There was music, a bar, tables, and lots of people and couples talking with other people and couples. Employees were visible taking drinks and crossing the dance floor. And no one was overtly having sex in the middle of room.

That was probably in another room, he supposed.

He decided to get a drink. He knew that was a good idea.

There were several seats at the bar and he sat down on the nearest stool. The bartender was a young man with several tattoos and piercings. Not Brunelle's type at all. He ordered a whiskey on the rocks and turned to look around again while he waited for his drink.

His eyes having adjusted to the not-dark-enough dark, he noticed a stage across the room, complete with a stockade and several similar devices pushed to one side. There was no show just then, but he wondered when the next one might be. With his eyes adjusted, he also noticed there was at least one couple in one corner either wrestling or having sex. He couldn't quite tell the genders from across the room, which just made him more curious. He didn't realize he was staring.

"They should get a room," the bartender said as he handed Brunelle his drink. "I mean really. We have rooms upstairs."

Brunelle looked at the bartender, not surprised as much as interested. He wondered what else might be upstairs.

The bartender nodded toward the couple in the corner. "That what you're into?' he asked.

Brunelle squinted across the room again. "Not sure what that is," he admitted. "But they seem to be enjoying each other."

The bartender chuckled. "Yeah, but they need to knock it off or go upstairs. We have rules."

Brunelle looked again. "Is that two guys?"

The bartender nodded. "Pretty much. One of them is trans. The other guy is into that. Looks like a girl, fucks like a man. Is that your thing?"

"No!" Brunelle snapped. A bit too emphatically, he realized. "No. I'm straight." Like that wasn't obvious. Forty-something dude drinking at the bar and staring at the other patrons. He probably looked like a cop. Not that far off, he supposed. "I mean," he added quickly, with a nod toward the corner couple, "not that there's anything wrong with that."

But the bartender disagreed. "Actually there is. They can't do that shit in public. That's why there's rooms upstairs. We don't need some undercover cop citing us for lewd conduct." He stepped out from behind the bar. "I'll be right back."

The bartender made quick work of the situation. On the way over, he swung by one of the several workers who were walking around with bowls full of condoms, grabbed a handful, and then stepped between the amorous couple. No small feat given the complete lack of space between some of their body parts.

Distribution of the condoms and a few gestures later, the couple was heading for the stairs and the bartender was heading back to Brunelle.

"Sorry about that," he apologized.

"No worries," Brunelle replied. He kind of found it interesting. "So undercover cops come here sometimes?" He found that interesting too.

The bartender shrugged. "Some of the neighbors think we're a nuisance. Like any place, there are bad apples who come. Drugs and fights and shit. We have rules but we have to enforce them. Otherwise some narc in street clothes suddenly flashes a badge and we're shut down for two weeks while the cops decide if we can reopen."

Brunelle looked down at his own street clothes. "I'm not a cop," he felt compelled to say.

The bartender laughed. "Oh, yeah. I knew that. You're way too uncomfortable. The cops who come here are all pervs. They love it. They spend an hour watching and touching and shit, and then at the end suddenly pull out the badge and cite us for all the shit they were just participating in. No, you're just another middle-aged guy looking for a thrill that may or may not be here."

Fuck. Brunelle would have preferred being mistaken as a cop. He hated being figured out.

"So why are you here?" the bartender asked. "You said it wasn't the trans thing. You bi-curious? That happens a lot with guys like you. If you want, I know a couple guys who are really gentle with newbies…"

"No!" Brunelle waved his hands at the bartender. "No, that's not it. It's, um…" But he paused. He felt compelled to explain why he was there, if only to confirm he wasn't interested in guys. Not that there was anything wrong with that. Still, he felt a little uncomfortable just telling the bartender. Like he was ordering another drink. 'I'd like some bondage on the rocks, please.' Instead, he managed to say, "Uh..."

He tried to figure out how to explain it without sounding like the dirty old man the bartender obviously thought he was—and he himself was wondering he might be. But before his mouth could find the right words, his eyes beheld the right image.

Coming out from a back hallway behind the bar was the most beautiful woman Brunelle had ever seen. Well, maybe not the most beautiful face, or body, or hair. But the most beautiful outfit. Or an outfit that made her the most beautiful. His heart nearly fainted, it started pumping so hard at the sight of her.

She was young. Too young. Half Asian, half something else, with broad cheekbones and thin eyes. Exotic. Her black curly hair was pulled back severely into a loose knot of a bun. Her frame was poured into a leather bodice that ended just above the complete lack of panties she was wearing. Black boots with such high heels that her feet were pointed almost straight down, like a ballerina on point. On her wrists were padded leather cuffs with silver rings hanging from them, and around her throat was a black leather collar, with matching silver metal rings at the front and sides. It was so thick it forced her chin into a permanently raised position.

"Uh..." he repeated.

The bartender followed his gaze to the gorgeous woman entering the area. He smiled, but Brunelle barely noticed—his eyes still adhered to the Aphrodite in Leather.

"So that's your thing," the bartender said. "Okay, yeah, I can see that. You have that vibe, I guess. But don't hold your breath over that one. She's owned."

That was enough to tear Brunelle's gaze away. "Owned?" he questioned.

The bartender nodded. "Yep. She's owned. By another one of our regulars. And you don't want to cross him. He's big and not afraid of violence. He doesn't mind if you look—in fact he kind of likes it—but don't touch. In fact, don't even talk to her. You talk to her, you'll be talking to him. And you don't want to talk to him."

Brunelle was about to say something about not being afraid to talk to anyone, and words being his weapon of choice, and something else equally insipid. But before he could, the lights went on and the clientele scurried for the corners like so much vermin.

"Police!" came a shout from the front door. "Party's over, folks. We're shutting this place down tonight."

A man ran out from the back and up to the two uniformed officers who had invaded the sanctum. He was obviously some sort of manager. "What are you doing?" he demanded, rather bravely, Brunelle thought. "You can't just barge in here like this."

But the shorter officer raised his hand to push the man back slightly. "We don't care what your patrons do to each other in the privacy of your establishment, sir, but when they start selling drugs, we can't just look the other way."

"Sell drugs?" the manager replied. "What are you talking about? Where?"

"A neighbor reported a drug transaction in the alley behind the club," the taller, thinner officer answered. "When we arrived there was a man in the alley with a fresh needle in his arm. He said he bought the drugs in here."

The manager literally shook with anger. "You stormed into my club on the word of a heroin addict? Are you crazy? I'll have your badges."

But the cops weren't impressed. "And we'll have witness statements from everyone inside the club. If there were drug transactions in here, someone saw something. And if someone saw something, your business license is in jeopardy, sir."

The threat to the manager was obvious. The one to Brunelle less so, but he understood it completely. When they came to take his statement, he could honestly tell them he didn't see anything. But he couldn't honestly tell them his name was 'Andrew Brown.' That would be the crime of False Statement to a Public Servant. Only a misdemeanor, but probably more than enough to get fired from being a prosecutor. But if his real name ended up in a police report...

"I need to get out of here," he turned to the bartender. "Now."

The bartender didn't miss a beat. And he didn't ask any questions. He just nodded, then gestured toward the door behind the bar. Brunelle moved quickly, especially for a dirty old man, and darted through the kitchen area to the door to the alley. A moment later he was outside. A moment after that, he was running down the dark alley, as far away as he could get from The Opal Room.

A few minutes later, he made his way back to the main road, his shoes soaked from the alley's puddles and his lungs burning from the cold night air. He didn't have to worry about ending up in a police report, but that wasn't what he was thinking about. He was thinking about the woman in leather. Maybe it was good the cops had busted in. He probably would have ignored the bartender and tried to talk to her. And bravado aside, her master likely would have kicked his ass six ways to Sunday.

Still, the image of the woman was burned into his brain and it wasn't going to leave lightly. He looked up at the street signs and got his bearings. His car was back by the club, so he'd have to walk. But it wasn't that far. He could walk to get to what he needed. Who he needed,

When he finally arrived, he was damp from the rain and exhausted from the walk. But he was driven on by the urge coursing through his veins. He pounded on the door a little too loudly. It was late. Past bed time for good people.

It took a minute or two, but eventually Brunelle heard the

deadbolt unlock and the door opened to him.

"David?" Kat was already in her pajamas—flannel, with a matching robe over them. "What are you doing here? You said you were working late tonight."

Brunelle ignored the question. He stepped forward, grabbed her firmly by the back of her neck, and looked deep into her eyes. "I need you, Kat."

Kat took a moment, but then smiled and pulled Brunelle inside.

CHAPTER 19

The close call with law enforcement distracted Brunelle from further curiosity about Seattle's sex club scene. The ensuing night with Kat, and the several nights following that, distracted him from his curiosity about Robyn. And the imminent hearing on Jacobsen's motions to suppress, redress, and dismiss distracted him from Yvonne Taylor's efforts to disbar him. By the time he walked to Judge Quinn's courtroom for the motions hearing, Brunelle was singularly focused on seeking justice, defending his prosecution from Jacobsen's frivolous attacks, and celebrating his inevitable victory that night with Kat.

So running into Robyn in the hallway was triply devastating. Or rather, her sly whisper as he passed was. "Andrew Brown?" Her little giggle was the icing on the focus-shattering cake.

"Wh-what?" Brunelle choked, his hand frozen on the courtroom door handle. Then, sure he was blushing and damning himself for it, he tried, "Is that a new client of yours?"

The giggle unfolded into a headshaking laugh. "No, Dave. You left before the cops could arrest you."

Brunelle didn't immediately respond, unsure of how to, and that was confirmation enough for Robyn. "I'm friends with the bartender," she explained. "He told me about this good-looking guy in his forties, checking everything out like a kid in a candy store, then bailing out the back door when the cops arrived. I actually wasn't positive it was you until now. Your face is redder than a paddle-spanked ass cheek."

Brunelle still couldn't find any words, but he smiled slightly. *She said I was 'good-looking.'*

"Good luck with your motions, *Andrew*," she laughed. Then she lowered those lids again. "And you don't have to go to all that trouble. My offer is still open."

With that she walked away and left Brunelle to try to regain himself somehow.

He closed his eyes, took a deep breath, and opened the door to the courtroom. The sight of Jacobsen and Atkins sitting at the defendant's table almost, but not quite, forced out the mental image of Robyn's paddle-reddened ass cheeks.

"Mr. Brunelle!" Jacobsen called out upon seeing him. "Good to see you again."

Brunelle wasn't so sure. But he said, "You too," anyway.

"Are you ready for round one of our motions?" Jacobsen went on. "You could just concede the first one, you know. Then the rest of them would become someone else's problem."

Brunelle nodded. The first motion was to disqualify him from the case for his alleged misconduct in speaking directly to Atkins. Although superficially tempting—he had plenty of other work to do—there was no way he was going to just concede it and walk away. It would be a terrible precedent to set that a defendant could bump a prosecutor off his case just by filing a bar complaint.

"Thanks," Brunelle replied, "but I think I'll stay. I like this case."

Jacobsen grinned over his client's nodding head. "Oh, I know you do. And I know why."

Brunelle felt the blush sear his cheeks again. Did they know about The Opal Room? What he'd done with Kat? What more he wanted to do with Robyn?

"Because my client is innocent," Jacobsen explained. "And what greater victory for a prosecutor than to convince a jury to convict an innocent man?"

A lopsided smile creased the side of Brunelle's face. Ordinarily, he would have been offended by the suggestion, but the relief that Jacobsen was just being an asshole, rather than knowing about his recent escapades, tempered the irritation.

"Sorry, Ron," he replied as he stepped over to the prosecutor's table. "Prosecutors seek justice, not just a conviction. I have no interest in convicting an innocent man. But your client is anything but innocent."

At that moment, Yamata broke the threshold of the courtroom. All eyes turned to the attractive young attorney as she pulled open the door with a bang and hurried to Brunelle's side, her arms full of files and books.

"Sorry I'm late," she panted as she dropped the books onto the prosecutor's table.

Brunelle looked up at the clock. It was 8:57. Three minutes until the hearing was scheduled to begin.

"You're not late," Brunelle observed. "In fact, you're right on time."

But Yamata shook her head as she straightened out her books and files and notepad into perfect order before her. "No. Early is on time. On time is late. And late is unacceptable."

Brunelle looked at her for a moment and another lopsided smile graced his features. He knew she was serious, and there was no point in arguing with her. So instead he asked, "Ready?"

Her materials in place and the clock about to strike 9:00, she smoothed her hair back and smiled. "Ready. Get ready to be dazzled by the force and eloquence of my oral advocacy."

"All rise!" the bailiff announced. "The King County Superior Court is now in session. The Honorable Susan Quinn presiding." And Judge Quinn emerged from her chambers to take the bench.

Brunelle had been pleased when they drew Quinn for the trial. He knew all the judges and all the judges knew him, but not all the judges knew Yamata. Quinn had been the judge on the trial Yamata and Brunelle had done together—Yamata's first murder trial. Brunelle had found that it was impossible to be in the same room with Yamata and not be impressed by her. After how Yamata had handled herself in that last trial, Brunelle figured Quinn felt the same way.

Which was good, since Yamata was going to be arguing the motions to dismiss for prosecutorial misconduct. He could hardly protest his own innocence credibly. He needed his own lawyer.

"Are the parties ready to proceed with the motions hearing?" Judge Quinn asked from her perch above the attorneys.

Jacobsen stood to address the court. "Mr. Atkins is ready." Brunelle noted Jacobsen's use of his client's name rather than 'the defendant.' Smart. Humanize him.

Yamata stood up next. "The State is ready."

Brunelle frowned slightly. No chance to humanize him. Prosecutors didn't have clients—just 'the State' or 'the People' or 'justice', whatever that meant.

Quinn looked over to Jacobsen. "These are your motions, counsel. I'll hear from you first."

Jacobsen nodded and Yamata sat down. She patted Brunelle's arm. Just in case he didn't already feel like he was on trial. He glanced over to Atkins, perhaps expecting a knowing look from a kindred spirit, but Atkins was paying attention to the proceedings. Brunelle figured he should probably do that too. He looked up at Jacobsen and steeled himself for the onslaught of personal attacks. He suddenly recalled that lawyers can't be sued for slander for things they say in court.

"May it please the court," Jacobsen began formally. "Mr. Atkins has brought forth several motions regarding misconduct by the government, and specifically by Mr. Brunelle. This misconduct has prejudiced my client, has deprived him of due process, and has made it impossible for him to receive a fair trial. At a minimum, the court should remove Mr. Brunelle from the case, but in truth the entire prosecution has been tainted by his malfeasance and the only just remedy is dismissal."

Quinn raised her hand slightly. "Let me interrupt you, counsel. I've read your briefing. As I understand it, you're alleging that Mr. Brunelle violated the Rules of Professional Conduct by having contact with a represented person, correct?"

"I'm not alleging anything, Your Honor," Jacobsen replied. "It's uncontroverted that Mr. Brunelle spoke directly with my client. He concedes as much."

Quinn looked over to Brunelle, who shrugged and nodded in reply.

"The State concedes the contact," Yamata stood to say, "but we disagree that it violated the RPCs or in any way prejudiced Mr. Atkins."

Judge Quinn clicked her tongue. "I'm sure it prejudiced Mr. Atkins to some degree. Everything prejudices every party to some degree. But I think there are two separate issues here. One is whether Mr. Brunelle may have violated his professional ethics. The other, and frankly the one I'm more concerned about, is whether Mr. Brunelle somehow violated Mr. Atkins' constitutional rights."

She tapped a finger against her lips and Jacobsen was experienced enough to wait for the question that was obviously coming.

"Mr. Jacobsen, do you think Mr. Brunelle's questioning violated your client's right to remain silent?"

Oh, fuck, Brunelle thought. He hadn't thought of it that way.

Obviously neither had Jacobsen. But he liked the idea. "Uh, well, yes, that's an excellent question, Your Honor. I would have to say yes. Mr. Brunelle is a state actor and he interrogated my client without advising him of his right to remain silent. That would appear to be a violation of *Miranda* rights."

Brunelle knew there was a flaw to that argument, but it didn't jump immediately to mind. He looked to Yamata, whose brow was likewise creased in incredulity, but Quinn spoke before either of them could quite tease it out.

"I agree that Mr. Brunelle was a state actor," she said. "He's the prosecutor. But *Miranda* only applies if the interrogation is custodial. Was your client in custody at the time of the contact?"

Brunelle was suddenly very glad that Atkins had made bail.

"Uh no, Your Honor," Jacobsen admitted with a bit of a squirm. "He had posted bail. But there was the lingering chilling effect of having been unjustly incarcerated."

Brunelle almost managed not to roll his eyes at that. *The bondage master chilled by physical restraint. Right.*

"And there can't have been a violation of his right to counsel," Quinn interrupted, "because Mr. Atkins' previous attorney was there representing him, isn't that correct?"

"Well, his previous attorney was physically present," Jacobsen sneered, and glanced back at Atkins, "but I would hardly say that he represented my client's best interests."

Quinn allowed herself a smile and a nod. She knew Lannigan too.

"Are you suggesting then," she asked Jacobsen, "that although your client was no longer physically in custody, the prior detention, coupled with the threat of reincarceration upon conviction, rendered the conversation quasi-custodial? And further that Mr. Lannigan, by acting in concert with Mr. Brunelle, took on the role of a *de facto* government actor, thereby converting the conversation into a type of custodial interrogation for which a formal advisement of *Miranda* rights was required?"

Jacobsen paused. Then smiled. "Yes. That."

Quinn nodded and pursed her lips. She looked over to the prosecution table. "Ms. Yamata, does the State intend to introduce at trial anything Mr. Atkins said during that interview?"

Yamata considered the question and looked to Brunelle. He could barely remember the conversation. He didn't remember any bombshells. Whatever Atkins said then, he likely already said the night of the homicide, after Chen had properly advised him of his rights. Brunelle shook his head.

"No, Your Honor," Yamata related.

"Good," the judge said. "Then the issue is moot. The remedy for a constitutional violation is the suppression of the evidence obtained from that violation. The fruit of the poisonous tree. The State has said they do not intend to introduce any statements from that conversation, therefore I don't need to decide whether there was any violation." Then she unfurled a thin smile at Jacobsen. "Although I will say that I think the argument quite attenuated."

Well, that's a relief, Brunelle thought. But it wasn't quite that simple.

"I think Your Honor might be missing our point," Jacobsen interjected.

Brunelle winced. Don't tell a judge she missed your point.

Quinn's smile, however thin, faded completely. "Oh?" she asked, in as icy a tone as that single syllable would allow.

"Y-Yes," Jacobsen stammered. He understood the tone. "We aren't seeking mere suppression of some pieces of evidence. Mr. Brunelle violated the Rules of Professional Conduct and thus—"

"Isn't that an issue for the Bar Association?" Quinn interrupted. "Not the trial judge in the criminal case?"

"Well, I think it impacts the criminal case," Jacobsen persisted, "but yes, the Bar Association has been notified."

Quinn pushed herself back in her chair. "You filed a bar complaint?" she demanded.

Thank you, Brunelle thought. *At least someone else is indignant about it.*

"Ah, my client did," Jacobson replied weakly. "Not I."

Quinn cocked her head at him. It showed her disbelief without saying anything that the court reporter could actually take down for future review.

"So there's a pending bar complaint against Mr. Brunelle for exactly the conduct you're alleging here?"

Jacobson thought for a moment, then nodded. "Yes, Your Honor."

Quinn looked directly at Brunelle. "Were you aware of this, Mr. Brunelle?"

Brunelle nodded. "Acutely."

The judge looked back to Jacobsen. "And what happens to Mr. Brunelle if I make a finding that the alleged misconduct occurred?"

Jacobsen paused and offered his own thin smile. "I suppose he will face discipline."

"Suspension?" Quinn pressed.

Jacobsen shrugged. "Possibly."

"In which case, he'll no longer be the prosecutor on this case," Quinn observed.

Or any case, Brunelle knew.

"I suppose not," Jacobsen agreed.

Quinn looked again to Brunelle. "Have they assigned an investigator yet?"

Brunelle finally stood to address the court. "Yes, Your Honor. Yvonne Taylor. I had the pleasure of meeting her recently."

"I bet," Quinn muttered. Jacobsen drew in a breath to say something but she stopped him with a wave of her hand. Then she steepled her fingers together and pressed them against her lips in thought.

After several moments, she announced, "I have heard nothing that requires suppression of evidence or otherwise directly impacts this particular criminal case. To whatever extent Mr. Brunelle may be facing professional discipline, that is a matter best handled by the Bar Association. I decline to interfere or prejudge that investigation. Accordingly, I am reserving ruling on the motion to dismiss for misconduct until the Bar Association completes its investigation."

The lawyers all took a moment to absorb what the judge had said.

"The Bar is unlikely to complete its investigation until after the trial in this matter," Jacobsen protested.

Quinn nodded. "I agree."

"So what happens if the Bar finds misconduct after the trial?" Jacobsen asked.

"Then I will reconsider the motion to dismiss. If Mr. Atkins is acquitted," Quinn explained, "the motion will be moot. And if he's convicted, I will consider vacating that conviction if the Bar finds misconduct on the part of Mr. Brunelle. Just because the jury says 'guilty' doesn't mean I have to impose a conviction."

"So we try the entire case knowing you might throw out the conviction anyway?" Brunelle half-complained.

Quinn looked down at him like a loving, but irritated mother. "Would you rather have me throw it out now?"

I'd rather have you find I didn't commit misconduct, Brunelle thought, *and forward that finding on to Yvonne Taylor*. But he knew not to say that. In fact, he knew not to say anything more at all. "No, Your Honor. Thank you, Your Honor."

CHAPTER 20

"I'm not exactly dazzled," Brunelle commented as they left the courtroom. "Your arguments seemed a bit lacking."

Yamata shot daggers at him from the corner of narrowed eyes. "I never got to my arguments. Quinn barely even talked to me."

"She barely talked to anyone," Brunelle expanded Yamata's comment. "But at least she didn't dismiss the case."

"Not yet," Yamata complained. They'd reached the elevators. She banged the 'up' button way too hard, way too many times. "But now we've got your stupid bar complaint hanging over our heads the entire trial. Why the fuck should we try the damn thing if it's just going to be dismissed afterwards because of your unethical ass?"

Brunelle wasn't unaccustomed to profanity, and Yamata wasn't one to avoid it, but she usually kept her emotions in check. She was pissed.

"Yeah, sorry about that," he offered. "But I really don't think we need to worry too much. It's a bullshit complaint. They'll dismiss it once they really look into it."

"Sure," Yamata replied as the elevator doors opened. "If it

were so cut and dry, why haven't they dismissed it already?"

Brunelle frowned. That was a good question. Yvonne Taylor didn't seem to think it was so cut and dry. In fact, she didn't seem to like him. Peter Sylvan liked him. Too bad he wasn't a real bar investigator. Then again, what he did seemed a lot more interesting…

"Are you even listening to me?" Yamata spat. "Jesus, Dave. We have a trial in less than a month on a national-news sex murder and the entire time we try it, there's a risk it gets dumped anyway. Can't you think of anything to say?"

Brunelle thought for a moment. "It's a manslaughter case, not murder."

"Fuck!" Yamata slammed the file into Brunelle's chest. "You need to figure this out. I am not putting all that effort into a trial if it's just gonna get pulled out from underneath me at the end. I have enough regular trials I can lose just fine without you and your ethical problems."

Brunelle took the file and also the abuse. He knew she wouldn't really ask to get off the case. She was ambitious. Ambitious prosecutors don't ask to get taken off of high-profile cases. Still, she had a point.

"I'll call the bar," he said calmly. "Maybe they can expedite the process. I'll explain what the judge just ruled. I really didn't do anything wrong. Looking back, I wish I hadn't done it. But I followed the rules. Really."

Yamata's angry visage softened. The elevator doors opened again and they stepped off into the hallway. She pulled the file back from Brunelle. "Okay. I bet they will. Get in there and get this settled. I want to convict this bastard."

Brunelle nodded. He did too.

Yamata finally cracked a smile. Slight, but definitely extant. "You're unusually quiet, Dave. Especially with me yelling at you and all. Nothing else on your mind?"

    You're fucking gorgeous when you're angry. But he knew better than to say that.

    He returned the controlled smile. "Let's get this guy."

CHAPTER 21

"You want to be interviewed now?" There was no disguising the surprise in Yvonne Taylor's voice. But over the phone, Brunelle couldn't tell if her jaw had dropped in astonishment, or she was licking her chops in anticipation. "Most attorneys try to draw out our investigation as long as possible."

Brunelle nodded. "Yeah, defense attorneys do that too, hoping the witnesses will lose interest or move away. Ordinarily, I'd be happy to put this off as long as possible—after I retire, say— but something's come up."

"Oh?"

Brunelle could tell by the tone of that one syllable that her expression, whatever it had been, had changed to one of curiosity. She was an investigator, after all. He had her.

"Yeah," Brunelle started. "It's like this..."

So Brunelle explained the judge's ruling, or rather, her lack of ruling. He explained the impact a delayed bar investigation could have on a hard-fought conviction. And he explained that he felt confident he would be exonerated so couldn't they just get it done with?

When he finished, there was a long pause. He decided not to

fill it. After a few more moments, Taylor asked, "Are you available to come to the Bar offices next Thursday at nine a.m.?"

Brunelle quickly pulled his calendar up on his computer screen. He had two pre-trial conferences and a motion to continue trial date all scheduled that morning.

"I'm wide open," he said. Yamata would cover those hearings for him too. Ambitious young lawyers don't say no to covering court dates for senior attorneys.

"See you then, Mr. Brunelle," Taylor said.

"Looking forward to it," Brunelle lied. They both hung up and Brunelle wondered again whether Taylor was smiling like the cat who was about to swallow the canary.

* * *

Yamata was relieved Brunelle had scheduled his interrogation so quickly. She was doubly so when they got served with Jacobsen's scheduling order. He hadn't been kidding about 'round one.' After losing that round—or not winning it anyway—Jacobsen pushed on to the more troubling motions: attacking the case itself. Brunelle's meeting with Yvonne Taylor was set for a Thursday. The following Monday morning he and Yamata would be back in front of Quinn, trying to explain why she shouldn't just throw the case out. It was an accident, Jacobsen would argue, and even if everything the State alleged were true, it still wouldn't be a crime.

Ordinarily judges denied those types of motions—known by the lawyers as *Knapstad* motions, after the Washington case where the trial court actually did throw out a case. But this wasn't an ordinary case. Both sides agreed that it was an accident. That's what manslaughter was, an accident. But Brunelle would argue to the jury that it was a preventable accident, Atkins should have known better, and therefore it was a crime.

Normally all a prosecutor had to do to defeat a *Knapstad*

motion was just stress that the jury should decide the case, not the judge. But given the touchy motion to dismiss she was going to have to deal with after a trial, Quinn could wash her hands of the whole thing by ruling that no reasonable jury could possibly find Atkins guilty for the accidental strangulation of his willing sex partner, dismiss the case, and punt the misconduct claims squarely to the Bar.

So when Brunelle walked into the lobby of the Washington State Bar Association that Thursday, the stakes were even higher than just his bar license. If he could get the complaint dismissed before the hearing on Monday, Quinn would relax a bit and do what judges are supposed to do: get out of the lawyers' way and let the jury make the decision.

He greeted the receptionist and took a seat in the steel-and-glass decorated lobby, trying not to look anxious. But he was definitely distracted—he hadn't even noticed whether the receptionist was attractive. He thumbed absently through the latest issue of the Bar News, waiting for Taylor and taking some solace in his preparation. He wasn't an expert on the Rules of Professional Conduct. But he was an expert on evidence, and what it takes to prove somebody did something they shouldn't have.

"Mr. Brunelle?" Yvonne Taylor stepped into the lobby from the hallway leading back to the interrogation chambers. Brunelle looked up from the magazine he wasn't reading. There was no question Taylor was attractive.

He stood up and dropped the magazine on the table. "Ms. Taylor." He made sure to match her level of formality. He'd have returned an 'Yvonne' if she'd led with 'Dave.' "Thank you again for expediting this meeting. I think it will prove fruitful."

A half smile creased Taylor's mouth. "Maybe," she offered, crossing her arms. Then she uncrossed them again and gestured into the bowels of the bar offices. "This way, Mr. Brunelle."

Lamb to the slaughter, Brunelle thought. But he was thinking about her.

Taylor's office was the same glass and steel furniture, with professionally matted diplomas and certificates looming on the wall behind her. The photos on her desk were of her in various national parks, hiking and generally exuding the prototypical Northwest Woman. He noticed she was alone in all the pictures. *Good*. There were also none of some guy or of any kids. *Even better*.

A comment about her vacation photos would be too transparent. A compliment about her appearance would be too unprofessional. But he needed her to like him enough to be open to dismissing the complaint against him. A defense attorney friend once confided after one too many drinks—it was professionally advantageous to socialize with friends on the other side—that he told his clients to say three things at sentencing: One, I'm sorry; two, I've learned from this; and three, it will never happen again. That's what the judge wanted to hear. The last thing any judge—or bar investigator—wanted was to cut somebody a break only to have that person go out and reoffend.

The punch line of the defense attorney's story was that he had worked out a sweetheart deal for an obsessive-compulsive client who was charged with stalking. The guy couldn't quite let go of his ex-girlfriend. At sentencing, the client knew what he was supposed to say but he opted to be honest instead. He said, 'I'm sorry. I've learned a lot. And I can *almost* guarantee this will never happen again.' The judge ignored the plea bargain and gave him the maximum sentence.

Brunelle leaned forward in his seat across Taylor's desk. "Thank you," he said, "for agreeing to expedite your investigation. I know it's not your normal procedure and I know you didn't have to do it. But like I explained, it really helps me out given what the judge ruled. I know you didn't have to do this, so I just thought I should tell you, no matter how this turns out, I appreciate the professional courtesy."

Brunelle could tell Taylor was smart enough to see through any disingenuous attempts at flattery. She deserved an honest thank you. He was smart enough to give it to her. Sometimes honesty was the best policy. It didn't help that stalker, but something told Brunelle it might well help him.

Taylor's reluctant smile told him he was probably right. She inclined her head slightly toward him. "You're welcome, Mr. Brunelle. Usually we do take longer to complete our investigations, but then again, usually the attorneys are in no hurry to be disciplined. This isn't the usual case."

Brunelle allowed a small smile onto his mouth. But he wore a huge grin inside. Lawyers deal in words. Words can deceive, but they can also reveal. Taylor had let slip two important facts.

First, she saw Brunelle's interview as a conclusion to the investigation. That confirmed what Brunelle suspected. Second, if most investigations delayed an eventual imposition of discipline, and his wasn't the usual case, that suggested there would be no imposition of discipline. The logical consequence from his suspicion.

The only question left in his mind was whether to hang back and respond to whatever Taylor decided to do, or go ahead and take the offensive. But there wasn't much of a question. He was a prosecutor. Prosecutors played offense.

"Mr. Atkins declined to be interviewed for your investigation, didn't he?" Brunelle started.

Taylor hesitated, sitting up slightly in her chair, as if both surprised by Brunelle's question and unsure how to reply. But then she relaxed again.

"No," she admitted. "His new defense attorney—"

"Ron Jacobsen," Brunelle suggested.

"Right," Taylor acknowledged. "Mr. Jacobsen indicated his client couldn't provide any further information, given the pendency of the criminal case. He urged us to take action based on Mr. Atkins' original written complaint."

I'm sure he did, Brunelle thought. He managed not to make a snarky comment like, 'How nice of him,' and instead moved on. "Mr. Lannigan didn't talk to you either, did he?"

Taylor had to smile a bit. "No. He expressed concern about the ethical implications of his own conduct."

Brunelle nodded. He figured Lannigan would be worried about his own hide. Or his own bar card.

"So really," Brunelle ventured, "you don't have any competent evidence I did anything wrong."

It wasn't about whether the defendant committed the crime. It was about whether the prosecutor could prove the defendant committed the crime.

Taylor's smile grew despite her obvious effort to stifle it. "I have Mr. Atkins' original complaint."

Brunelle waved his hand. "Rank hearsay."

Taylor actually laughed, in part because they both knew he was right. "I have your own admissions," she reminded him, "from when I came to your office."

Brunelle frowned slightly. She had a point. He enjoyed telling people that criminal suspects talked far more often than they invoked their right to remain silent. People were surprised. He'd stopped being so. But he was surprised just then to realize he'd been just as stupid with Taylor as all those defendants were with whatever detective was interrogating him. Everybody thinks they can talk their way out of a jam. It turned out he wasn't any different.

The frown morphed into a chagrined smile. "I don't think I admitted too much."

"You admitted to speaking with a represented party,"

Taylor replied.

Brunelle nodded. "Are you sure I didn't admit to speaking with his lawyer while he was present?"

Taylor just looked at him.

"You didn't record our conversation," Brunelle pointed out. "If I recall correctly."

That smile Taylor was fighting cooled a bit. "This isn't some criminal trial, Dave."

Dave. Perfect. He had her.

"No," Brunelle agreed. "It's far more serious. It's my bar license."

Another involuntary laugh. He was going to be out of there in fifteen minutes. Maybe ten.

Taylor raised an eyebrow as she considered his allocution. "I see you've thought this through," she admired. "But this isn't a courtroom and I'm not bound by the rules of evidence. You talked to a represented person. That implicates RPC 4.2."

"Implicates it," Brunelle agreed, seizing on the word, "but doesn't violate it. Courtroom or not, to prove an allegation there has to be evidence that a particular rule was violated, whether that's RPC 4.2 or RCW 9A.32.050." That was the statute for Manslaughter in the First Degree. Even sitting there defending his law license, that damn case was never really out of his head. "You don't have that evidence. Without Atkins and Lannigan, all you've got is me." He smiled innocently. "Cooperating fully with the Bar and in all ways the model attorney."

Taylor leaned back and steepled her fingers in front of her face—mostly to hide the full blown smile he'd elicited. "You're very confident in yourself, Mr. Brunelle."

Back to 'Mr. Brunelle', but it fit the sentence. It was still friendly. There were situations when he liked being called Mr. Brunelle. He could imagine even more—and who with. *Damn that case.* He shook his head ever so slightly to regain his focus.

"I'm confident in you, Ms. Taylor," he replied deftly. "Confident you'll look at all the evidence, or lack of evidence, and conclude that while I may have exercised poor judgment, there's insufficient evidence to find I actually violated any of the Rules of Professional Conduct." Time to wrap this up. "But I can tell you this: I'm sorry this happened, I've learned from it, and I'll never do anything like this again."

Taylor tapped her fingers against her pursed lips and regarded the man across her desk. Brunelle held her gaze, but tried to do so earnestly, rather than aggressively. Finally she leaned forward again and dropped her hands on her desk.

"I already decided just that," she announced. "Whenever a complainant refuses to be interviewed, we're likely to dismiss the complaint. Once the only other witness also declined to cooperate, I knew exactly what I was going to do."

Brunelle smiled, relief mixed with irritation. "Then why make me come all the way down here?"

Taylor shrugged. "I wanted to see what you had to say. I didn't think you'd go all trial lawyer on me, but you make a good point. Let me review the file one more time, then I'll send you a letter stating the complaint has been dismissed. You'll have it well before your trial."

Taylor stood up and so Brunelle followed suit. He extended his hand. "Thank you, Ms. Taylor."

She took it and smiled—finally just a relaxed, unfettered smile. "Call me Yvonne. And you're very welcome, Dave."

CHAPTER 22

Brunelle felt like celebrating. Fortunately, it was Thursday night and he and Kat had a standing dinner date at The Jade House in the International District. He was excited to share his triumph with her. He'd had a good day.

Unfortunately, Kat had had a shit day.

Her gait was a bit lumbering, her hair a bit disheveled, her expression a bit cloudy. None of which Brunelle noticed when she trudged up to the table where he was already seated.

"You're late," he grinned.

She didn't smile back. Brunelle wasn't a stickler for punctuality. He didn't like a concept that gave you sixty seconds to get it right, and everything else was either too early or too late. Ordinarily, he wouldn't even have noticed her late arrival, but he was eager to begin the celebration.

Kat, however, appeared anything but celebratory.

She didn't offer a witty rejoinder. Not even a tired, but good-natured, 'Fuck you, David.' Instead she just glowered at him as she dropped in to her chair. His heart tightened under her disapproving glare.

"Uh, so..." he stammered as he reached for the glass of water the bus boy had already brought. "I had a really good day today."

Kat looked up from the menu, but just barely. She raised her eyes, but kept her chin down, so she was practically looking through her eyebrows. "Ask me how my day was."

He really didn't want to. He wanted to tell her about his day. And there was no doubt she'd had a bad day. She was going to complain or worse about God knew what and he was going to have to pretend like he cared, like she was totally right, and like he was just as upset, or offended, or outraged as she was at whatever or whomever she was angry at. But then, he supposed, that came with being the 'boyfriend.' Being there for her, even when he'd rather be somewhere else. He took a sip of water, wished he had something stronger, and steeled himself. "How was your day?"

She slapped the menu onto the table. Brunelle just knew she hadn't picked anything. It was going to be forever before they ordered, longer before they ate.

"My day sucked," Kat started, "thank you very much."

Brunelle nodded. He already knew that. He also knew to shut up and let her talk.

"First off," Kat continued, "I woke up late. I never wake up late. But Lizzy... Oh God, David, be glad you never had kids. I don't care how cute they are when they're little, they grow into teenagers. She's got homework, grades, ...boys." That last word held especially noticeable venom. "And now she wants to go visit her dad, and well, you met him."

Another nod, but he didn't take the bait to criticize her ex-husband. He was familiar with the 'I can criticize my family, but you can't' dynamic and she was in a rare mood. He may have been stupid, but he was no fool.

"So anyway, we got into a big argument, and it just went on forever, and I was up way too late, then couldn't sleep, and I slept right through my fucking alarm. Lizzy slept in too since I didn't wake her up, so she missed the bus and I had to drive her to school which was just a joy considering the previous night's argument and the fact that that was the reason we were late in the first place."

There seemed to be a break in the narrative, one long enough to offer maybe a 'Yeah, that sucks,' but he stuck with the silence. It was safer.

"So I was over an hour late to work. Usually I get in before rush hour, but this morning I got stuck right in the middle of it. What the hell is wrong with the drivers in this city?" She shook her head at her own question and went on. "What the hell is wrong with everyone in this city? There were eight bodies waiting for me when I got in. Well, seven bodies, and one body bag full of miscellaneous remains that were half liquefied."

Brunelle grimaced slightly. He wondered if the other patrons could hear her. He also made a mental note to skip the miso soup.

"Then, when I finally get changed and into the examining room, Fenton is already doing one of my autopsies. One of *mine*."

"Yours?" Brunelle went ahead and asked. "Why was it yours? Do you guys call dibs the night before or something?"

Kat narrowed her eyes. "No. They get assigned out every morning by the director. Fenton had his list, I had mine. But he finished his first one before I got there, so he started doing mine."

Brunelle's brow knitted. "Maybe he was trying to do you a favor?"

Kat's own eyebrows lowered, but in a menacing way. "Fenton's a jerk. He doesn't do anybody any favors. He was trying to make me look bad."

Brunelle decided not to respond. He was pretty sure whatever he might say would be wrong.

"He'd go blab to everyone that he'd done all of his autopsies plus some of mine."

Brunelle ventured a syllable. "Oh."

"Exactly," Kat elected to agree. "So I told him to step away from the corpse."

"Did he?"

"After a second, yeah," Kat snarled. "Then he tried to hand me his scalpel, blade first." She paused for a moment. "Fucker."

Brunelle wasn't enjoying the dance, but he knew the music was still playing. "He should have handed it handle first, right?"

"He shouldn't have handed it to me at all," she replied like a mother disappointed with her child's denseness. "I don't want to use his fucking scalpel. I have my own, thank you. And yeah, he shouldn't have handed it blade first." She narrowed already angry eyes into near slits.

"Do you think he did it on purpose?" Brunelle asked, trying to keep up with her indignation.

But Kat scowled at him. "No, not on purpose," she spat. "Jesus, David, do you always have to be the prosecutor?"

That wasn't what he'd meant. He was just asking. He shook his head slightly. "Well, yeah. Sorry. I guess, I dunno." He wasn't sure what to say. "I guess that would have hurt, huh?" he offered with a shrug.

"Fuck the pain, David," Kat growled. "He could have stabbed me with a biohazard. The body — *my* body — was a homeless guy they found O.D.'d in an alley. I could have gotten TB, or Hep C, or even fucking AIDS."

Okay, yeah, Brunelle agreed in his head. *That would have sucked.*

"I would have had to go to the hospital," Kat went on, "to get a bunch of blood drawn and they would have put me on a cocktail of like ten fucking antibiotics until I was shitting water every thirty minutes."

Brunelle nodded. *Definitely no soup.*

"Well, look." Brunelle wasn't really sure why Kat was getting so upset about something that didn't actually happen, but he was starting to get tired of defending against ghosts. "I don't think—"

But Kat cut him off. "That's exactly right, David. You don't think. You don't know shit about what I do, but you think you do because you read autopsy reports. You think you know guns because you read ballistics reports. You think you know mental illness because you read psych reports. But really, everybody else actually does stuff and then you just glom on at the end and pretend you're part of it too. You can pretend you're a doctor, or a firearm expert, or a psychologist, but really you're just a lawyer. Maybe you should stop pretending you're something you're not and accept who you really are."

Brunelle didn't have to hold his tongue that time. He was speechless.

Kat seemed oblivious. She took a long drink of water, then finished her complaint. "I ended up working through lunch so I wouldn't be late for our fucking dinner, and to top it all off, Lizzy came home sick and so she's home alone now, still mad at me, and here I am with you."

Brunelle nodded weakly.

"So yeah, that was my day," she concluded. She picked up her menu again and finally started hunting for something to order. "What was so fucking great about your day?" she grumbled without looking up.

Brunelle's desire to share his victory had completely evaporated. He wasn't angry, but his joy was definitely gone. "Oh, nothing special," he lied. "I just got a lot done, is all. I was productive." He shrugged and smiled weakly into his water as he took another drink. "That makes for a nice day."

"A nice day," Kat scoffed as she lowered the menu and

glanced out the window. "Well, maybe you should go for a fucking walk," she joked darkly.

Brunelle looked at the door. There was nothing he'd rather have done right then.

CHAPTER 23

In the event, going for a walk was exactly what Brunelle did after dinner. The rest of the meal had been just as tense and unpleasant as the beginning. He listened and offered measured comments, but Kat was preoccupied with getting home to Lizzy, and Brunelle was eager to stop being another thorn in her day's side. He handed the waiter his credit card as soon as the food came and they were out of there in under an hour. Kat walked straight to her car and Brunelle walked up Jackson Street. Toward Capitol Hill.

He didn't really think about where he was going; it was just the opposite direction of the rest of the International District. Away from the waterfront. Uphill, so his legs burned. The better to think with.

There were a lot of different, interlocking thoughts, grinding in his head. Like mismatched gears. Different shapes and sizes, designs and materials, but each turning every other gear in the row as it spun.

Kat. Robyn. Boyfriend. Girlfriend. Lover, master, friend. Duty, desire, obligation. Want. Need. Love. Lust. Sex. Right, wrong, justice, ethics. Normal and aberrant. Satisfaction and frustration. Expectations and disappointments and regrets. And realizing you've reached your destination when you didn't even know you were on a journey.

Brunelle found himself In front of The Opal Room. It was late enough that the club was open but early enough that it was still empty. There was a flyer taped to the door.

MASQUERADE FETISH PARTY.

THIS SATURDAY.

CUM NOT AS YOU ARE

BUT AS WHO YOU WANT TO BE.

Brunelle's heart caught fire. She was going to be there. He knew it.

And he knew he would be too.

CHAPTER 24

Brunelle stayed in his office all day Friday. He only had one court hearing—a pre-trial on a run-of-the-mill gang shooting—but he sent Yamata to cover it. Ambitious young prosecutors cover preliminary hearings for senior prosecutors. And senior prosecutors who don't want to run into attractive young defense attorneys send ambitious young prosecutors to the Pit to cover their hearings.

It wasn't that he didn't want to see Robyn. Just the opposite really. But he didn't want to see her right there, right then. Not at the courthouse, not at work. If they ran into each other, it might break the spell. He might say something stupid. She might say something stupid.

Brunelle shook his head. *She wouldn't say anything stupid.*

But he might. Or she'd look at him in some way he didn't understand, and it would fluster him, and he'd lose his nerve. No, he needed to stay as far away from Robyn as humanly possible on Friday, so he could get as close to her as humanly possible on Saturday.

By the time Saturday evening came around, Brunelle was more than ready to find Robyn. And he was prepared. Well, as prepared as he knew how. A career as a trial attorney had taught him that sometimes you have to just go into uncertain situations and do your best. Walk into the courtroom even if you don't know what's going to happen. But it also taught him to be as prepared as possible before walking into the unknown. If he did run into Robyn, he wanted to be prepared. So he did what he always did before a big performance. He read up on it.

Geeky, he knew, to read up about sex. But it had paid off for him before. His first serious girlfriend had benefited from his checking out an anatomy book to determine, in advance, exactly where this thing called the 'clit' was.

So where his earlier reconnaissance mission had been cut short by the arrival of the police, his academic studies had proceeded uninterrupted. He remembered well enough where the clit was, but if he found himself with Robyn, far more experienced than him, he knew, he wanted to at least try to keep up with her expectations. He wanted to impress her. He wanted to satisfy her.

But first he had to find her.

The party had started at 9:00. Brunelle had considered waiting until 10:00, but the thought that he might miss his chance with Robyn got him there by 9:15.

A lot could happen in an hour.

There was a line to get in, but it moved quickly, and Brunelle soon found himself in a crowded, gyrating, pulsating room of costumed fetish enthusiasts. Not exactly his normal crowd. But he liked it. The mask covering his face helped. He'd spent a lot of time trying to decide on a costume. More geeky online research looking for a character from a movie or a book who might fit into what he was pretending to be. But then he decided to stop pretending he was something he wasn't. He just wore a black suit, white shirt, and skinny black tie he dug out of the back of his closet. A simple black mask over his eyes and nose and he was done. If you didn't know him, you wouldn't recognize him. And if you did know him... well, she'd know exactly who he was.

Brunelle pushed his way through the crowd. He recalled from his last trip that there were rooms off to the back, but a good portion of the crowd apparently didn't get the memo. Several couples were already engaged in various stages of, well, engagement. Brunelle looked away—not because he minded watching or they could possibly have expected any privacy, but because his masked eyes were scanning the room for Robyn. So he was completely unprepared for the woman who grabbed him by the tie and slammed him against the wall before shoving her tongue in his mouth.

He didn't resist, but he didn't reciprocate either. It was obviously not Robyn. Robyn was white. And after she pulled away and went back into the crowd for more, Brunelle realized she might not even have been a woman. Somehow that didn't bother him as much he thought it probably should.

He really needed to find Robyn.

And there she was, across the room, staring right at him.

"Fuck," Brunelle exhaled.

She was even more beautiful than he'd fantasized. He'd imagined every type of fetish fantasy costume. Leather, lace, thigh-highs, riding crops, but nothing matched what she'd settled on.

She was wearing a hospital gown. A sexy one, short, and open in the back, he knew. But that wasn't what was so perfect. It was the fake pen sticking out of her right cheek, right under the red leather mask barely covering her perfect blue eyes.

She wanted him to recognize her too.

Except for the pen, which had been extracted by the surgeons, it was what she was wearing when he'd seen her at her most vulnerable, and her most resilient. Her strongest.

She locked leather-rimmed eyes with him and smiled. The fake pen tipped up on one cheek and her dimple appeared on the other. He smiled too and stepped toward her. She didn't move an inch. She knew he'd come to her.

He did.

But when he got there and leaned in for a kiss, she dodged it. Instead, she grabbed his hand and led him away from the main room and its frenzied crowd, down the dimly lit corridor to the private rooms. She walked ahead, her back to him, his hand firmly held by hers. Sure enough, the hospital gown was open in the back. She was wearing thin lace panties, the same blue as her eyes, and no bra.

He watched the swing of her hips as they went, easily imagining the baby blue underwear dropping to the floor. The blood rushing in his ears matched the rhythm of the club's music. He felt simultaneously hypnotized and hyper-aware. They reached their room. Robyn let go of his hand long enough to unlock the door, then backed in, pulling him onto her as they spilled inside.

Brunelle barely noticed the furnishings. A sparse bed against one wall and a small table with some things strewn across it. But his attention was squarely on the woman in his arms. She pulled the fake pen off her face and threw it against the wall even as her mouth merged with his. His hand quickly undid the ties to her gown; hers made short work of his belt and his pants hit the floor almost as fast as her costume. They undid his shirt and tie together and fell onto the bed in nothing but their underwear, which was no barrier for probing hands.

Her grasp was firm and practiced, her body hot and welcoming. They didn't speak as their hands explored each other, tongues entwined, hearts racing. She kept her eyes open, staring into his in a way he'd never experienced before. It wasn't the mask that still surrounded them. It was the message they sent. 'Take me.' A command to be commanded. He could hardly do anything but obey.

He stood long enough to slide off his underwear. Robyn slipped her own off and leaned back onto the bed, opening her legs to him. A moment later he was on top of her. A moment after that he was inside her. As close as humanly possible.

She gasped when he pushed in, then grabbed the back of his neck and they quickly found their rhythm. Something about her made Brunelle feel bigger, stronger, more desirable than maybe he ever had. He buried his face into her hair and varied his pace to elicit more gasps and moans from his partner.

He was lost in the moment so was taken completely off guard when she reached down to his hips and pushed him out of her.

He jerked his head up. "What's wrong?" he panted. "Did I do something wrong?"

Robyn smiled into his eyes and shook her head slightly. "Nothing wrong, Dave."

He was glad for that, but still didn't understand. His expression said as much.

"Why did you stop?" she asked.

He was even more confused. "Because you wanted me to. I mean, you stopped me."

His heart was pounding. Her hands still held his hips. He was poised at her opening, one strong thrust from being inside her again, damn her hands. She leaned up and took his lower lip in her teeth. She pulled at it and let go, then looked into his eyes. "So?"

It took a moment for her comment to register. It took less than that for Brunelle to grab her wrists and pull her hands over her head. He held her wrists in place, stretching her lithe body taut, and pushed back into her, deeper than ever. She screamed. He smiled. He knew he wouldn't last. It didn't matter.

Soon after, spent, he let go of her wrists and pushed himself up and out of her. He laid down next to her and wrapped his arms around her waist. He was disappointed he'd finished so soon. He wondered if she was too.

As if reading his mind, Robyn rubbed her perfect, dimpled, scarred face into his chest and sighed. "Good start, Dave. Go ahead and catch your breath. There's no rush. I rented the room for the whole night."

She glanced to the table. Brunelle did too. Among the things she'd brought, he noticed a pair of handcuffs, one of the half-open manacles forming the shape of a heart.

She leaned up and kissed his chin even as her hand slid lower to see if he might ready again soon. "We have a lot to do tonight."

CHAPTER 25

Much like how he felt about his initial performance with Robyn, Monday came sooner than Brunelle would have liked. It wasn't just that he was worried about the outcome of the hearing on Jacobsen's motion to dismiss. He'd lost plenty of motions in his career. But he didn't want to have to do it so publicly. The courtroom was packed. Sex sells, even in the courthouse. Duncan was skipping the festivities—a little too lurid for an elected official—but Fletcher and Jurgens were there. Chen too, and a couple of the other detectives who had assisted on the case. And Jessica Edwards. And hiding in the back, behind the newbie prosecutors and local reporters, was Robyn Dunn.

Brunelle had the class not to wink at her. It had been an amazing night, but he wasn't exactly sure where they stood. Luckily he was distracted when a further scan of the room led to another familiar face, one he was genuinely surprised to see again. At least right then.

"Dr. Sylvan." Brunelle inclined his head to the defense expert in the front row. "Good to see you again."

More curious than good, but Brunelle didn't really mind the sexologist's presence. He was feeling pretty non-vanilla after his night with Robyn. "Here to watch the show?"

But Sylvan grinned. "I'm not really into watching," he quipped. "Unless it's research. I'm here to participate."

Brunelle cooked his head. "Participate?"

Sylvan smiled and nodded. "Yes, I'm here to testify."

Brunelle frowned. But he didn't reply. There was no testimony at that type of motion to dismiss. It was what the lawyers called a 'Knapstad motion,' named after the case that established the procedure. It was basically a 'Is that all you got?' motion. The defense concedes all the State's evidence and then argues that even if it's true, it's not a crime. Unfortunately, the case was a perfect candidate for just such a motion. Jacobsen could concede everything and then argue it was just an accident, not a crime. The standard was whether any reasonable jury could find that a crime had been committed. If the judge didn't think so, she would dismiss the case. The good news was all Brunelle usually had to do to defeat the motion was implore the judge to just let the jury decide. If they acquit the defendant, fine. And if they convict, that's proof that a reasonable jury could find a crime. Why take it out of their hands?

So why had Jacobsen brought Sylvan to testify?

Brunelle walked over to the prosecutor's table and sat down. Yamata was already there.

"Did that guy," she asked, looking at Sylvan, "just say he's going to testify?"

Brunelle nodded, but didn't say anything, the gears in his mind turning.

"We're going to object, right?" Yamata confirmed. "You don't get to call witnesses at a Knapstad motion."

Brunelle nodded again. "I know." But he didn't answer her question.

"So we're going to object?" she repeated.

Brunelle wasn't sure. He was getting an idea.

Judge Quinn entered then and everyone in the courtroom stood up until she announced, "You may be seated."

Jacobsen and Atkins had been whispering to each other during Brunelle and Yamata's conversation, but Jacobsen was paying full attention when Quinn asked, "Is the defense ready to proceed on its motion to dismiss?"

The defense attorney stood to address the court. "Yes, Your Honor. Our witness is present and ready to testify."

Quinn's eyebrow shot up. "Witness?" She knew the law too.

"Yes, Your Honor," Jacobsen quickly replied. No doubt he expected resistance and was prepared. "We believe Dr. Sylvan's testimony is necessary to show why no reasonable jury could possibly find this tragic event was anything other than an accident."

Quinn pursed her lips. "If the jury needs a witness to explain it," she tested, "doesn't that mean that the jury should make the decision?"

Yamata nodded, but Brunelle sat stock still. Preliminary motions weren't just about keeping the case alive. They were also about preparing for trial. Even assuming Brunelle won the motion to dismiss, Sylvan was going to testify at the trial and he was going to tell the jury it was an accident. Unless Brunelle could effectively cross examine him. And what better way to prepare his cross than a dry run? Besides, Brunelle was cocky enough to think he might actually be able to change Sylvan's mind. Then Atkins wouldn't even have an expert at trial.

Brunelle stood up. "The State has no objection to Dr. Sylvan testifying at this hearing. So long as the State is allowed to cross examine him."

Yamata grabbed his coat sleeve and whispered what every lawyer in the room was thinking. "What the hell are you doing?"

But Brunelle kept his eyes on the judge as he whispered down to his co-counsel, "Trust me."

Yamata let go of his arm and pushed back in her chair. It was pretty obvious she didn't trust him at all. But it was his case.

Quinn didn't seem to trust him either. "Are you sure, Mr. Brunelle? I wouldn't ordinarily allow testimony at this type of hearing."

Translation: object and he won't get to testify.

"I'm sure, Your Honor," Brunelle replied. "The State has confidence in its case."

"Too much confidence," he heard Yamata mutter.

Quinn hesitated, then shrugged. "Very well. There being no objection from the State, I will allow Dr. Sylvan to testify. I've already read the pleadings and was prepared to receive argument from the lawyers. Shall we move directly to Dr. Sylvan's testimony?"

Brunelle and Jacobsen both agreed and Sylvan stepped forward to be sworn in.

"What the hell are you doing?" Yamata demanded in Brunelle's ear as they sat at counsel table. "We win this motion on the pleadings. Whether it was an accident or not is the jury's call. But you're letting the defense expert tell the judge that no jury could possibly do this. Are you trying to lose so the Bar will get off your back?"

That stung. "Wow. No." He whispered back. "No. And I already got the Bar off my back." He had been about to explain to her what he was doing, but he lost the desire to bring her on board. "I know what I'm doing." Then, to put her in her place, "This is my case."

Yamata wasn't really one to be put in her place, but she huffed and crossed her arms. "Your case. Your funeral. I'm not taking any blame for this fuck up."

Brunelle nodded. *Fine,* he thought. But he suddenly doubted his decision ever so slightly and really hoped it didn't turn out to be a fuck up after all.

"Please state your name for the record," Jacobsen began his direct examination.

"Peter Sylvan." The sexologist had a relaxed air about him. Confident, with just a trace of arrogance. Perfect for an expert witness.

"Are you familiar with the case at issue here today?"

Sylvan nodded. "Yes. I have been retained by the accused as an expert."

Jacobsen nodded. He had a three-ring binder open on the bar and was working through his obviously prepared direct exam. He wasn't even looking at Sylvan. But everyone else in the courtroom was.

"And what is your area of expertise?"

"I'm a sexologist," Sylvan replied, fully expecting the titter that washed through the gallery. "I hold a bachelor's degree in psychology and human sexuality from the University of Michigan, and a master's degree in sexology from Seattle State University."

Jacobsen looked up from his binder long enough to acknowledge the awkwardness of the topic with an uneasy smile. But it was the nature of the case. The human thing to do was to be slightly embarrassed. The lawyerly thing to do was to press on.

"And do you have a particular sub-specialty?" Jacobsen asked, returning his gaze to his notes.

Sylvan nodded, then looked up to the judge to answer. "I specialize in nonreciprocal power relationships and restraint protocols."

Jacobsen looked up to see if the judge got it. Her expression was difficult to read, so he followed up. "Sado-masochism?" he tried to clarify.

Quinn's eyebrow raised enough to signal her understanding of that term. But Sylvan expanded. "That's one dynamic," he answered. "There are others. Not all involve actual infliction of pain. There's a broad variety of activities people engage in."

The murmur through the gallery was more subdued. Scholarly interest, perhaps, rather than juvenile tittering.

"Have you had a chance, Dr. Sylvan," Jacobsen continued, "to review the police reports in this case?"

"I have," Sylvan replied. "I also reviewed the crime scene photographs and the autopsy reports."

"So are you familiar with the circumstances surrounding Christina Belfair's death?"

Yes," Sylvan answered. He was about to expound but Judge Quinn cut him off.

"As am I," the judge said. "As I said, I've reviewed the pleadings, which included the relevant police reports so I could assess whether a jury could possibly convict Mr. Atkins. I don't want to spend time having this witness recount the details of the death here. I assume," she looked to Jacobsen, "this witness has more to offer than a recitation of the facts?"

"Yes, Your Honor," Jacobsen replied. He turned to Sylvan. "Based on your education and experience, and your review of the reports in this case, do you have an opinion as to whether *any* rational jury could possibly find Mr. Atkins guilty of manslaughter?"

Yamata jumped to her feet. "Objection!"

Brunelle looked up at her, wide-eyed. Apart from everything else, Sylvan was *his* witness. Only *he* was supposed to make objections. Now Quinn could force Yamata to do the cross exam, which would defeat the entire purpose. "What the hell are you doing?"

"What the hell are *you* doing?" she whispered back. "You can't let this guy give that kind of opinion. We don't have a responsive witness—because there aren't supposed to *be* any witnesses. The only record for the judge will be Sylvan's opinion and she'll have to grant it."

Brunelle didn't fully agree with that analysis—that's what cross examination was for—but he could see her point.

"Will Ms. Yamata be doing the cross examination?" Quinn asked. That was enough for Brunelle to dodge that bullet.

"No, Your Honor," he replied before Yamata could. "I'll be doing the cross. Just a little communication problem. My apologies."

Yamata glared at him but didn't say anything.

"Are you objecting?" Quinn asked.

Brunelle hesitated. Yamata raised her eyebrows at him and gave an animated nod. Brunelle frowned. He didn't like to object, but Yamata's concern was valid.

"We do object to that particular question, Your Honor," he said. "It's for the court to decide whether any reasonable jury could find the defendant guilty. That's a legal conclusion and Dr. Sylvan's area of expertise is, well, not the law anyway."

A light laughter passed through the gallery. Brunelle thought he saw a smile crack the corner of Quinn's mouth as well.

"I think he could give his own opinion as to whether a crime occurred," Brunelle continued, "but he shouldn't be allowed to do more than that."

Quinn nodded thoughtfully and looked to Jacobsen. "Any response?"

Jacobsen also nodded thoughtfully, but regardless of the logic of Brunelle's objection, Jacobsen was still an advocate first. "There's no rule against a witness providing an opinion as to the ultimate issue. When he testifies at trial—" Then he corrected himself. It was important to be confident about his motion to dismiss. "That is, if he *were* to testify at a trial, then he would give the opinion Mr. Brunelle is trying to limit him to here. But the question before the court is whether any jury could possibly find my client guilty and that is the question I want him to answer."

Quinn pursed her lips in thought for several seconds. Finally, she sustained the objection. "I'll determine whether any jury could find Mr. Atkins guilty. This witness should limit his testimony to his own opinion on Mr. Atkins' guilt. Please rephrase your question."

Jacobsen frowned. But the difference between what he wanted to ask and what he was being allowed to ask was pretty thin, especially after a discussion that made it obvious what Sylvan would have said if he were allowed to answer the original question. "Yes, Your Honor," Jacobsen deferred to the judge. He returned his gaze to his witness. "What is your opinion as to whether Mr. Atkins is guilty of any crime in relation to Ms. Belfair's death?"

Sylvan nodded, finally allowed to speak. "Based on my expertise as a sexologist, and my review of the relevant law enforcement reports, and the relevant statutes defining the crime of manslaughter, it is my opinion that Mr. Atkins is not guilty of any crime. This was an accident. A fatal accident, to be sure, but an accident nonetheless."

Jacobsen closed his binder and smiled at his witness. "Thank you, doctor. No further questions."

All eyes turned to Brunelle. Especially Yamata's. And, he knew, Robyn's. If he were honest to himself, he had to admit part of his reason for wanting to cross Sylvan was to show off to Robyn what she'd taught him during their night together.

He stood up and took his place as the cross-examiner. Close enough to the witness to suggest confrontation, but far enough away to not be a jerk about it. There was no jury to impress anyway.

"Good morning, Doctor," he began. "Nice to see you again."

Sylvan smiled. "You too. How's the practice?"

That stunned Brunelle for a moment. *Wow, what an ass*, he

thought. He was going to enjoy the cross exam.

"Oh, you know," he offered his own grin. "Learn something new every day."

Sylvan raised an eyebrow. His curiosity apparently overcame his antagonism. Brunelle pressed his advantage.

"So you're an expert in BDSM, correct?"

Sylvan nodded carefully. "Correct."

"And that stands for bondage, discipline, and sado-masochism."

Another careful nod. "Correct. I'm an expert on all aspects of human sexuality, but those are my areas of focus."

As much fun as it might have been to explore the details of that area of focus out loud in a crowded courtroom, Brunelle knew the best cross examinations were the shortest. Select your opening and hit it hard. So to speak.

"And although those practices are," he looked to the ceiling for the right word, "atypical, they are enjoyed by a large number of people, correct?"

Sylvan gave a more honest nod. "Yes. The numbers vary, but it is a substantial portion of the population. Many people don't talk about it because of the stigma associated with, as you said, atypical sexual practices."

Brunelle braved a glance back at Yamata. Her expression was incredulous. 'What the hell are you doing?' was pretty clearly written across her features. Brunelle turned back to his witness.

"In fact," he said, "those practices are common enough that there are several companies which manufacture, um," another glance to the ceiling, "equipment, correct?"

"Oh, yes," Sylvan replied. "There is no shortage of 'equipment' for people who wish to enjoy themselves that way."

"Equipment specifically designed for nothing but that type of sex, right?" Brunelle pressed. "Not just rope and handcuffs, but very specific things that have no other possible use?"

Before Sylvan could answer, Judge Quinn interrupted. "Is this going somewhere, Mr. Brunelle?"

Brunelle looked up to the bench. "Uh, yes, Your Honor."

"Can we get there quicker?" the judge encouraged.

Brunelle nodded. "Yes, Your Honor. Just a few more questions. I'll get to the point."

Quinn leaned back. "Thank you."

Brunelle turned back to Sylvan. "And these devices, they're readily available?"

Sylvan had to agree. "Yes."

"Manufactured by corporations that would get sued if they made anything that ended up hurting anyone?"

Sylvan's nod was practically in slow motion as he finally understood where Brunelle was going. "Ah, well, I don't know about that exactly…"

"But instead of using any of that equipment, Mr. Atkins chose to rely on standard rope and his own knot-tying abilities and now Tina Belfair is dead, isn't that correct?"

"Objection." Jacobsen stood up with an air of fatigue. "That's a compound question."

Quinn looked down at Brunelle. "He's right. And you made your point." She crossed her arms. "Are we there yet?"

Brunelle looked to Yamata. She actually looked pleased. It was a nice look on her.

"Yes, Your Honor," Brunelle answered. "No further questions."

"No redirect, correct, Mr. Jacobsen?" Quinn's question was clearly anything but. Jacobsen acquiesced.

"Ready for argument, Your Honor," he replied.

Then both attorneys gave their arguments, Jacobsen maintaining it was a tragic accident, Brunelle blaming Atkins' poor rope skills. By the end, the gallery was full of whispering, and Quinn's eyes were full of relief that the hearing was finally over.

"Thank you, counsel, for that," she looked to the ceiling herself, "*educational* hearing. But if there's one thing I've learned from this, it's that this is obviously a very complicated area, full of facts not generally known to the average person. We can all agree that the death of Ms. Belfair was tragic. But I will let the jury decide whether it was a crime. The motion to dismiss is denied."

Brunelle pumped his fist ever so slightly and looked to Yamata.

She shrugged but smiled. "I guess you knew what you were doing after all."

The judge adjourned the case and everyone stood up to leave. As Brunelle was gathering his things, Sylvan stepped up. "Well done," he said. "I thought you were going somewhere else with that line of questioning."

"Oh yeah?" Brunelle asked. "Where?"

But Sylvan just smiled. "Somewhere else." Then he nodded to Yamata and took his leave. "See you at the trial, counsel."

Jacobsen was still crouching over the defense table huddling with Atkins, so Brunelle skipped the professional nicety of saying 'good job' or 'goodbye' and instead followed the crowd out into the hallway. He craned his neck to spy Robyn in the back of the courtroom but she was already gone. His heart sank at the thought that she had missed his brilliant cross exam, but it was buoyed again when he saw her in the hallway. She was leaning against the opposite wall and looking right at him as he exited the courtroom, but before he could walk up to her, he was accosted by several reporters and at least three news cameras with blinding lights activated.

One of the reporters shoved a microphone in his face. "How did you manage to win that hearing?" she asked. "The defense expert seemed to think it was pretty black and white."

Brunelle recognized the reporter from Atkins' arraignment. Unfortunately it stirred up slippery memories of their first encounter, and in his victory haze, he spoke without thinking. "Most things aren't black and white. In this case, Mr. Atkins is fifty shades of guilty."

He immediately regretted the quip, but the cameras were rolling and he knew it would make the air by the way the reporter squealed at getting the sound bite that had eluded her earlier. In fact, as soon as they got the audio, they were done with him. They turned off their camera lights and raced after Jacobsen and Atkins who had tried to sneak out the other way.

Yamata was about to make some undoubtedly sarcastic remark when she noticed Robyn waiting for him. So instead she said, "I'll meet you upstairs, Dave. We can debrief and map out our next steps to prep for trial."

She gave Robyn a parting nod and headed for the elevators. The rest of the crowd had also dissipated, leaving Brunelle and Robyn alone together in the hallway. Robyn pushed herself off the wall and stepped over to him.

Forcing his sound bite blunder out of his mind, he smiled at her. "So what did you think of my cross?"

Brunelle expected accolades. Maybe even a proposition. Instead, Robyn slowly shook her head at him, a disappointed smile creasing the corner of her mouth.

"I think," she said, "you didn't learn a damn thing."

CHAPTER 26

The phone rang. Even as he answered it, Brunelle thought maybe he shouldn't have.

"Fifty shades of guilty?" It was Kat. "What the hell kind of quote was that?"

Brunelle peered at the clock on the other side of his apartment. It was 6:07. The news must have led with his comment. It was before the first commercial anyway.

"A stupid one," Brunelle answered. "I wasn't thinking."

"It was funny," Kat admitted. "But not very professional."

"I know."

"You're going to get in trouble, aren't you?"

Brunelle lowered his head into his hand. "Yeah. Probably."

"With who?"

"Matt," Brunelle started. "Judge Quinn. The victim's family. Jacobsen. Pretty much everybody."

"What about the Bar?" Kat asked.

Brunelle frowned. He'd snatched defeat from the jaws of victory. No amount of charm and small talk was going to get him out of that one. "Yeah, them too. Prosecutors aren't supposed to make comments like that to the media."

Kat laughed lightly. "Just the jury, right?"

Brunelle smiled weakly, even if Kat wasn't actually there to see it. "No. I'm pretty sure the Court of Appeals wouldn't like it either."

There was a pause. Then Kat asked, "So what were you thinking? You're usually good with the media."

He shook his head. "I don't know. I guess I was just jacked up from winning the hearing. I... I don't know."

But he did know. He just didn't want to tell Kat.

Kat paused again, then asked, "Do you want to come over tonight? Lizzy's here, but it's not like she doesn't know what we do. Some company might do you good."

But that was the last thing he wanted to do. He felt guilty enough for letting Yamata and Duncan down by making that statement. He didn't need his guilt compounded by seeing Kat face-to-face only days after being with Robyn.

"Thanks," he said, "but I think I just want to be alone tonight."

Another pause. "I'm sorry about dinner last week," Kat said. "I had a really shitty day and I took it out on you. That wasn't fair of me."

And neither was that apology, thought Brunelle. He'd needed the resentment he'd felt that night to help him justify what he really couldn't justify. An apology was just going to make it worse. "No worries," he said. "Nothing to apologize for. I have shitty days too."

Kat chuckled. "Like today."

Brunelle shrugged. "It was good except for that stupid sound bite." He was thinking about winning the hearing. Then he thought about what Robyn had said afterward, and how she'd turned and walked away from him after saying it. "Well, mostly good. I guess."

They were both quiet for a few moments, then Kat said,

"Well, I think I'm going to let you go. You don't seem like you really want to talk, and I'm not gonna be a bitch and force myself on you. But don't beat up on yourself. You're a really decent guy. Everybody makes mistakes."

Brunelle grimaced. If only she knew. "Thanks, Kat. Have a good night."

"You too," she replied. "Call me tomorrow?"

Brunelle nodded to himself again. "Sure." Then, "Yes. Sounds good."

They hung up and Brunelle leaned back on his couch. What a shitty day. And suddenly Saturday night—which he'd initially thought of as one of the best nights of his life—had perhaps become one of his worst mistakes. He knew Robyn would keep her mouth shut. He wasn't so sure he could.

He sat there for several minutes, his thoughts and emotions swirling in his head. Finally, he picked up the phone and dialed.

"Hello?" Kat answered.

"Is that invitation still open for tonight?"

He couldn't see it, but he knew she was smiling. "Yes. Of course."

He hesitated. "Are you sure she knows what we do?"

Kat laughed. "She's in high school, David. She knows."

"I've had enough public humiliation today," he said. "Do you think you can be quiet?"

"I can be whatever you need," she purred.

Brunelle knew that. He just wished he would have remembered it earlier.

CHAPTER 27

Brunelle got to work early the next morning. It had been a nice night. Nothing fancy, or acrobatic, or 'atypical'. Sometimes vanilla can taste pretty good.

But whatever lingering afterglow he took with him to the office disappeared when he checked his voicemail.

"Hey, Dave, it's Larry. Saw you on the news. Great quote. Hilarious. All the guys down here loved it. Uh.... you weren't supposed to say that, were you?"

Beep.

"Mr. Brunelle, this is Yvonne Taylor from the Washington State Bar Association. We will not be dismissing your grievance after all. In fact, we'll be opening a new file based on your comments to the media. I strongly encourage you to retain an attorney and have them contact me as soon as possible."

Beep.

"Dave. This is Matt. Come to my office as soon as you get in. I think you know why."

Beep.

He lowered his head into his hands, then pushed his fingers through his short, graying hair. "Could this get any worse?"

"Yes," came the unexpected reply. It was his secretary Nicole, darkening his door with a document in her hand. She stepped into the office and tossed the paper on Brunelle's desk.

He looked down and read the caption: 'Defendant's motion to dismiss for prosecutorial misconduct.'

Brunelle frowned. "Well, damn."

"Yeah," Nicole laughed darkly. "You're fifty shades of fucked."

CHAPTER 28

The courtroom was actually more packed than for the last motion. Sex sells. So does humiliation. Combine them into one prosecutorial train wreck, and a crowd was guaranteed. Where Brunelle had been glad to see Robyn at the last hearing, he was relieved she hadn't bothered to come to this one.

Especially when Judge Quinn took the bench.

Usually a judge will call the case, ask the attorneys if they're ready to proceed, then invite the moving party to begin. Quinn did none of that. She sat down and pointed right at Brunelle. "What is wrong with you?"

Brunelle grimaced. This was going to go even worse than he'd thought.

"Uh..." he started. Several thoughts flashed through his mind. The first was how criminal suspects were always told they had the right to remain silent. The second was that they almost never did. The third was that he used their non-silence to send them to prison. Lesson: shut up and don't admit shit. But he also thought about his professional obligations. Honesty in dealing with others. Candor to the tribunal. And all the cases he had where it didn't matter whether the defendant talked to the cops or not; all the other evidence proved he was guilty, witnesses, trace evidence, even video. Surveillance video. Or television video.

Sometimes the only thing you can say is sorry. "I apologize, Your Honor. It wasn't intentional."

"Of course it was intentional," Quinn fired back. "You can't form a sentence accidentally. Not a coherent sentence. Not that sentence."

Brunelle nodded. She was right. He'd said it intentionally. He just didn't intend the consequences. "You're right, Your Honor. I just meant that I didn't think before I spoke. I didn't mean to jeopardize the case."

"Never mind jeopardizing your case," Quinn snapped. "What about jeopardizing Mr. Atkins' right to a fair trial? Did you forget about that?"

Brunelle thought for a moment. Honesty. Candor. "Yes, Your Honor. That's exactly what happened. I forgot."

There was a tense silence for several seconds as Quinn scowled down at him. Finally Jacobsen cleared his throat and stood up.

"Would the court like me to articulate the basis for our motion?" he asked.

But Quinn shook her head. "No, counsel. Your brief is more than adequate. The Court is fully aware of the import of Mr. Brunelle's misconduct."

Great, Brunelle frowned. *Officially labeled as 'misconduct.'* Robyn wasn't there, but he wondered if Yvonne was. He didn't turn around to look. He had enough happening in front of him. And to the side of him, Yamata was sitting stony and silent. He imagined she didn't want to get painted with the same broad brush.

Quinn turned back to Brunelle. "Tell me why I shouldn't dismiss this case right now."

That was the whole issue, Brunelle knew. He'd known he

was going to get a public spanking—although he hadn't expected it to be quite this harsh. And he knew he was going to be seeing more of Yvonne the Inquisitor. But none of that mattered. What mattered was the case. What mattered was Tina Belfair.

"Because Mr. Atkins killed Tina Belfair," he said, "and she deserves justice."

It was an aggressive response to a judge, but what the hell. He didn't have much more to lose.

"My client deserves justice!" Jacobsen interjected.

Quinn glowered at him. She was delivering the spanking. "Your client deserves a fair trial," she corrected. "And it's my job to ensure that." She turned back to Brunelle. "And you, Mr. Brunelle, have severely damaged my ability to do that."

So that was why she was so pissed. She was taking it personally.

"Trial is in two weeks, Mr. Brunelle. Court administration has already sent out the jury summonses. We knew we might need extra jurors for this given the pretrial publicity. But now, two weeks from trial, you make some stupid comment that's gone viral. We summoned a hundred jurors just for this case. How many will we need now to find twelve who haven't been impacted by the publicity and your asinine comment? Two hundred? Three hundred?"

Brunelle shrugged. "I don't know."

But she had just handed him his way out. It was a small crack, but the door was open.

"And again, I apologize for the trouble my mental lapse has made."

"It wasn't just a mental lapse," Quinn corrected. "It was a professional lapse."

Brunelle could hardly disagree. "Yes, Your Honor. And I apologize. Your Honor has known me for some time now and knows that I don't try cases in the media. I take my professional obligations seriously and I had a momentary failing. A moment of weakness. I admit it and I apologize. But the court should deny the motion to dismiss anyway. At least right now."

Quinn's expression hardened, but there was a glimmer of curiosity in her eyes. "Why?"

"For exactly the reasons you said, Your Honor." It was always smart to butter up the judge when telling her why she should do something she didn't want to do. "Because this isn't about me. It's about Mr. Atkins' right to a fair trial. My comment was ill-advised, but it only becomes relevant if it impacts Mr. Atkins' trial rights. I can do all sorts of ill-advised things. I can park in a handicap spot. I can text while driving. I can cheat on my girlfriend."

Oh my God, why did I say that?

"B— But none of those matter," he regained himself quickly, "because they don't affect Mr. Atkins' right to a fair trial. And we don't know yet whether my stupid, asinine comment did either. It may impact my standing with the bar, or my reputation generally— both of which I deeply regret—but the only way it impacts Mr. Atkins is if we can't pick a jury who was unimpacted by my comment. And the only way to do that is to bring in as many potential jurors as possible and at least try to seat an impartial jury."

Quinn frowned and crossed her robed arms, but she didn't say anything immediately. Brunelle knew that was good for him.

So did Jacobsen. "There's more to the inquiry," the defense attorney inserted. "Mr. Atkins is prejudiced either way."

Quinn looked to him and raised an inviting eyebrow.

"The only way for me to discover whether a potential juror has been impacted by Mr. Brunelle's misconduct," he explained— Brunelle never thought he'd prefer being called asinine, but it was better that misconduct—"is for me to ask the juror. And the only way for me to ask the juror is for me to repeat Mr. Brunelle's asinine comment."

Much better, Brunelle thought sardonically.

"And if by some chance we do get a juror who hasn't heard it," Jacobsen continued, "I myself will make sure the juror does hear it by asking the question in the first place. That puts Mr. Atkins in the untenable position of having to either make sure everyone on the jury has heard the comment by asking about it, or picking a jury without knowing who might have heard it because I didn't want to repeat it. That is patently unfair. It is incurable. And the case should be dismissed."

Fuck, Brunelle thought. He had a good point. A glance at Yamata confirmed she thought so too. She'd lowered her face into her hands.

Both prosecutors looked up to the judge. The judge frowned down at them.

But no judge wants to dismiss a murder case. And Brunelle had given her an out. Again.

"It seems entirely possible that Mr. Brunelle's comments to the media may have made it impossible for us to seat a fair jury," Judge Quinn started. "But it will be impossible to determine that until we at least try. I will order the clerk of the court to summon another hundred potential jurors. I think perhaps we overestimate how carefully the general public pays attention to the news. Perhaps we'll be surprised by how easily we can find twelve people who weren't tainted by Mr. Brunelle's stupidity."

Brunelle grimaced at the characterization, but was glad for the ruling.

"Thank you, Your Honor," he said—barely resisting the urge to follow up with, 'May I have another?'

CHAPTER 29

A few days later Brunelle finally ran into Robyn. He was waiting for the elevator when she came out from one of the hallways to the courtrooms. She was wearing a dark suit with a knee length skirt. He noticed because she usually wore pant suits. And because he always noticed her. He liked how the suit hugged her curves even though he'd seen those curves without anything but his hands hugging them.

His greeting got caught is his throat as his eyes got caught on her soft red locks. So she spoke first.

"I heard about your hearing in front of Quinn," she said. "I guess you can talk your way out of anything."

Brunelle grinned. A stupid school boy, the cute girl is talking to me grin. He shrugged. "I guess so."

"How'd ya manage it? From what I heard, you totally should have had your case dismissed."

The specificity of the question allowed him to focus on the answer, rather than the body he knew was hidden beneath that dark suit. "I just accepted what had happened and why we were there. I screwed up. I have a role in the system and just fell short. But I realized that didn't mean anyone else had to drop their role.

Jacobsen had to bring the motion. He has an obligation to his client, so I didn't get mad at him. And Quinn has a job to do too. I made her job harder. So I acknowledged everyone's role in the system and explained why we could still go forward without anyone compromising their obligations."

Robyn listened intently to his answer. Then, after a moment, she smiled slightly and shook her head. "You have so much potential, Dave. And you don't even know it."

* * *

The elevator had come at that point and Brunelle went up to his office while Robyn headed for the exit. He knew he should feel bad about having cheated on Kat with Robyn, but he couldn't manage any feelings of regret right then. Instead, he was focused on the awkwardness of the encounter with Robyn and memories of her body against his. The last thing he wanted to think about was the ethics of it all so he was doubly annoyed when Kat texted him.

Dinner? Read the text.

Ugh, he thought. 'Dinner' usually meant more than just dinner. Except last time when it meant less. When it meant a not-quite-argument, and a walk, and a flyer, and eventually doing that 'more than dinner' with someone else. He stared at the text. Just like 'dinner' meant more than dinner, a 'no' might mean more than just a no to dinner. His fingers hovered over the screen, but he hesitated.

His lack of immediate response apparently prompted an encouragement text: *I found this great new restaurant. You'll love it.*

He sighed. Then typed.

Sounds great. Let's say 7:00. I'll meet you there. What's the name of the restaurant?

He watched his screen and waited for the response. Then, with a clench of his heart, he suddenly guessed what the restaurant would be just before it flashed on the screen: *The Pond. c u there. <3*

The heart was the perfect touch. Just fucking perfect.

* * *

Brunelle tried to beat Kat there. Maybe, if he was lucky, he could get that same secluded table. And tell the waiter there was an extra tip in it if he brought the food fast and the check faster. But that just reminded him that the wait staff might recognize him. In the event, it didn't matter. Kat was already there and had grabbed a table right near the entrance. Where any beautiful young defense attorney might walk in and reasonably conclude he had taken her romantic restaurant and commandeered it for another relationship.

"David!" Kat waved at him when he walked in. "Over here."

Maybe he could fake a stomach flu or something. He waved back and stepped over. "Hey, you." Then with a glance around the restaurant, he added, "Nice place." Like he'd never been there.

He sat down and tried to look around the way a person who had never been there before might do it. He picked up the menu that was already on the table.

Oh, look! A menu.

"Isn't this place amazing?" Kat enthused. "I just heard about it. I never knew it was here. It's totally hidden." She lowered her eyelids at him. "The perfect place for a clandestine rendezvous."

Brunelle forced a smile over the panic. "Yeah."

Good. Short simple responses. Like what he always told his witnesses about getting cross-examined by the defense attorney: answer the question, but don't elaborate.

Kat glanced down at her menu. "So how was your day?"

For a moment, he considered giving her a taste of her own medicine and answering, 'My day sucked,' just to do it. But that would have been petty. And besides, his day was fine.

"Uh, good," he said. "Nothing special."

Kat looked up long enough to nod, then back down to the menu.

It took him a moment, then he remembered to ask her too. "Uh, how was your day?"

The whole thing felt forced. He didn't like that. It had always felt natural with Kat. More than natural. But not then. Not any more.

She looked up again and smiled. "Fine. Cut up some bodies. Nothing special."

An awkward silence followed while Brunelle perused the menu without actually reading anything and glanced around in a way he hoped looked casual to see if he spied the waiter from his last visit. He didn't.

Kat set her menu down. "What are you going to have?" she asked him.

"Hm?" he pulled his thoughts back to where he was, and who he was with. "Uh, I don't know. Maybe the garlic chicken again."

Kat raised an eyebrow. "Again?"

Fuck.

He shrugged as casually as he could muster. "Yeah, isn't that what I usually get when we go to an Asian place?"

Kat gave him a long, appraising look. Finally she asked, "Are you okay, David?"

Brunelle felt his heart tighten. There was no way he was going to let the conversation go down that path. So he took refuge in his work. "Oh, it's just this damn sex club case." He shrugged. "I know there's a way to crack it, but I know I don't see it yet."

"He killed his girlfriend," Kat replied. "How hard is that to prove?"

"I can prove that, no problem," Brunelle answered. "I'm just not sure I can prove it was a crime. He didn't mean to kill her. That sounds like accident, not manslaughter. I need to figure out why it's manslaughter."

Kat laughed. "Maybe you should have figured that out before you charged it."

Brunelle had trouble appreciating the joke. "Yeah, well, it looked different at charging. They always do. But I can tell there's something I'm missing. Something that will make the jury understand."

Before either of them could say any more, the waitress came over. Brunelle was relieved it was a woman—definitely not the man who waited on him and Robyn. They placed their orders. Kat got the curry prawns. Brunelle got the garlic chicken. Again.

After the waitress' departure, the conversation returned to Brunelle's case. He complained some more and was generally morose and irritable. That seemed to keep Kat at an arm's length, lest she start asking specific questions he didn't want to answer, or lie about.

But just as Kat's irritability had worn on Brunelle, so too did his mood impact Kat.

"Ya know," she said, standing up and dropping her napkin next to half eaten prawns, "I think I'm going to go to the restroom. Maybe you can use the time to get into a better mood."

But her admonition simply ensured the opposite. He didn't think she had much right to lecture him on being pleasant dinner company.

He sat and stewed for a few minutes, then pulled out his phone and checked for messages. He had a new text. From Robyn.

I'm willing to give you another chance. Lol. Interested?

His blood raced, and not to his brain. But before he could reply, Kat returned from the bathroom. He slipped the phone back in his pocket, the unanswered text burning a hole in his leg.

She sat down and leveled her eyes at him. "Are we in a better mood now?" she asked in a sickly sweet sing-song.

Brunelle didn't like that. He wasn't her child.

Honesty, he told himself. *And candor*. But then the lawyer in him kicked in. *Or a reasonable facsimile thereof.*

"So, um," he cleared his throat. He couldn't believe he was about to say what he was about to say. But he knew what he was about to do. What he already had done. And he didn't want to be dishonest about it. That didn't mean he had to tell her everything, but he couldn't pretend everything was the way it had been either. "I've been thinking…"

Kat's face screwed up into a tight, guarded expression. Brunelle was smart; there was no doubt about that. But he wasn't the type to go around 'thinking.' That was the kind of phrase someone used when they were about to say something bad. Something really bad.

"Yes?" she encouraged. But her eyes betrayed trepidation.

"Well, just…" He tried, but trailed off. "Well, I mean. I guess maybe I need some space."

He looked at her eyes briefly, then quickly glanced away. He didn't like what he saw there. He didn't like being responsible for it.

It was a lame phrase. 'Some space.' It didn't mean anything. It was breaking up without breaking up, wanting to see other people without admitting it. But its very ambiguity amplified its impact.

"Space?" Kat managed a half-laugh. "Well, it's not like we're married." She forced a smile onto her features, but it was hard. "You can have all the space you need, David. By all means. I don't want to scare away the life-long bachelor by being there for him, listening to his worries, sharing his victories, laughing at his stupid jokes. You want space? You can have it. You can have as much fucking space as you need. In fact," she stood up, "let's go ahead and start now. You can finish dinner on your own."

She wasn't crying, but she wasn't about to stay and let that happen, Brunelle knew. She stormed toward the exit. He would have tried to stop her, but really, he wanted her to leave. He wanted space. And time. To return Robyn's texts.

But when he pulled the phone out of his pocket, there was another text from her.

Never mind. On second thought, bad idea. Sorry.

Brunelle closed his eyes and tried to ignore the explosion of emotions inside him. "Well, fuck."

CHAPTER 30

The Kat-and-Robyn-less days dragged on, but eventually it was the night before trial. Brunelle found himself alone in his apartment. He didn't drink much, but when he did, it was usually whiskey. He poured some over a glass of ice and stepped onto his balcony.

He was farther away than ever from understanding how to win the case. It was an accident. Jacobsen was going to say that a hundred times, just in his opening statement, And Brunelle could hardly argue. It was an accident. It's just that it was also a crime.

But why?

He could explain the law to the jurors, but he could imagine their eyes glazing over as he spoke.

'A person is guilty of manslaughter in the first degree when he or she is aware of a substantial risk that death might occur and ignores that risk. In contrast, a person is guilty of manslaughter in the second degree when there is a substantial risk of death, and a reasonable person would be aware of that risk, but the defendant wasn't aware of the risk and such lack of awareness was a gross deviation from normal conduct.

'Now, criminal negligence isn't defined anywhere in any

statute, but we know it's higher than regular negligence—the kind you would see in a civil suit for damages. We just don't know how much higher. And a substantial risk is more than a regular risk, but again, how much more isn't really defined anywhere.

'Now, let's talk a little about the word 'recklessly'...'

Brunelle shook his head. That type of argument would be sure to both bore and confuse the jury. Bored juries don't feel a passion for justice. Confused juries don't convict beyond a reasonable doubt.

He took a drink and looked out at the small section of city visible from his balcony.

He thought about the case, turned it over in his mind every which way, like a Rubik's cube, trying to figure out the solution.

But there was another reason he was obsessing about the case.

He took another drink. Too much. It burned going down.

If he could keep his mind filled with the case, there wouldn't be room for Kat.

Or—and he damned himself for still thinking about her, but he couldn't help it—for Robyn.

CHAPTER 31

In the end, Jacobsen elected not to ask the prospective jurors about Brunelle's 'Fifty Shades of Guilty' comment.

On the record, he explained to the judge, "Given our Hobson's choice between inquiring into whether the jurors have been tainted by Mr. Brunelle's misconduct, and ensuring they are so tainted by so asking, we reluctantly choose not to raise the issue."

Off the record, he admitted to Brunelle, "This is a free shot for me. Like when the defense jumps offsides and the ball gets hiked anyway. The quarterback can send everybody long and throw for the endzone. If it's caught, it's a touchdown. If not, no worries. Just accept the penalty and replay the down." When Brunelle didn't immediately embrace the metaphor, Jacobsen explained, "There's no way the Court of Appeals lets any conviction stand after your comment. If the jury acquits, we're done. If they convict, it's coming back anyway."

Brunelle still didn't reply. Just a noncommittal nod that said, *Yep. You're saying what you're saying.* But he knew Jacobsen could be right. The best defense attorneys didn't just try to win; they planted seeds for the appeal. So, after a relatively uneventful and uncontentious jury selection, Judge Quinn seated twelve jurors and two alternates and adjourned until the next morning for opening statements.

When they reconvened, Judge Quinn confirmed there were no more issues from the attorneys, then brought in the jury and announced, "Ladies and gentleman, please give your attention to Mr. Brunelle, who will deliver the opening statement on behalf of the State."

CHAPTER 32

Brunelle stood up and surveyed the courtroom. It was packed. Every seat in the gallery was taken. More spectators stood shoulder-to-shoulder against the walls. A TV camera stood in one corner. Pointed directly at him.

Everyone was waiting for him to speak. Everyone wanted to know what he was going to say. This was his moment. Whatever he said, it was likely to be the one thing everyone remembered. He needed to make it count. He needed to take advantage of the fact that the prosecution always gave the first opening statement. He needed to seize the initiative and put Jacobsen back on his heels.

He needed to be powerful. There were few things more powerful than honesty. And candor.

He stepped in front of the jury and opened his palms. A practiced gesture—calculated, ironically enough, to communicate sincerity. If they were only going to remember one thing, he wanted it to be the truth.

"It was an accident."

A surreptitious glance out of the corner of his eye. If everyone had been wondering what he'd say first, they were dying to know what he'd say next.

"No one wanted Tina Belfair to die that night. Not Tina. Not the staff at the Cu-CUM-ber Club. And certainly not Michael Atkins."

He looked back to where Atkins was sitting. Not because he really wanted to look at Atkins, but because it made him look sincere in the front of the jury, and because he wanted to see if his opening was pissing off Jacobsen as much as he'd hoped it would. He was going to give the defense opening first—then rebut it. All before Jacobsen got to say so much as, 'Good morning.'

But the defense attorney was wearing a solid poker face. Brunelle turned back to the jurors and continued.

"The defendant loved Tina. They had been in a committed relationship for years. They enjoyed each other's company. And they shared common interests. But it was during one of those commonly shared interests that Michael Atkins accidentally killed the love of his life."

This next part was tricky. The sexual circus that surrounded Tina's death threatened to distract from the significance of the crime. Prosecutors need jurors who feel the weight of the wrong and yearn to help right it. Distractions were always bad. Titillating distractions were worse. Titillating distractions that provided defenses to the charges were the worst.

"I'm not going to get into all the details of their relationship right now. You'll hear plenty of testimony about the sorts of things Tina and the defendant enjoyed doing together. But ultimately, those things don't really matter. What matters is that Tina Belfair is dead. And she's dead because of the conduct of Michael Atkins."

Brunelle took a moment to gather his thoughts and let the jury know that the next bit was important. There were few things worse than listening to a lawyer talk. Brunelle knew that. He never understood the attorneys who delivered three-hour opening statements. Openings were supposed to preview what the evidence would show. The longer you talk, the more you're promising the jury things you might not be able to deliver. And more importantly, you're boring the hell out of them. Get in, get to it, get out.

"It's important to understand that the defendant never intended to kill Tina. He is not charged with murder. He's charged with manslaughter. I won't get into the definition of manslaughter right now. That's not appropriate for opening statement. At the end of the trial, the judge will instruct you on the elements of manslaughter, and you will decide whether the State has proved each of those elements beyond a reasonable doubt, but for now it's important to note one thing. Manslaughter is an accident. And manslaughter is also a crime.

"You see," he opened a professorial hand to the jury, "just because something was an accident, doesn't mean it isn't also a crime. Mr. Atkins didn't mean to kill Tina, but he did. And he had an obligation to be more careful than he was. If you back up your SUV in a crowded parking lot and run over a child, that's an accident. If you knew there were kids around, and you knew someone could be hurt, and you went ahead and backed up anyway, that's manslaughter. If there's a substantial risk someone could get killed, and you disregard that risk, it's more than just an accident. It's a crime."

That was the crux of it. Accident or not, Atkins was guilty. He'd given them the roadmap, the outline. He just needed to fill it in a little with some detail and he'd be done. It wasn't quite enough to tell the jury that Tina died because Atkins messed up. They needed to feel it.

"The night Tina Belfair died, she was helpless. Her hands and feet were bound and her mouth was gagged. The defendant wrapped a rope around her throat. She could do nothing to save herself, or even tell the defendant she was in distress. Immobilized and unable to speak, she slowly suffocated to death even as her friend and lover stood by, oblivious to what was happening. Oblivious to what he had done. Just like the man who backs up his SUV in a parking lot full of kids, Michael Atkins should have known better. And in fact, he *did* know better. He knew there was a substantial risk Tina could die from having her breathing so restricted. But he didn't care. He had his own needs to attend to."

A subtle dig at Atkins. Overdue, really.

"And while he attended to those needs of his, and he disregarded the risks to his lover, Tina Belfair died."

Time to wrap it up.

"No one wanted Tina Belfair to die that night," he repeated. "Not Tina. Not the staff at the Cu-CUM-ber Club. And certainly not Michael Atkins. But just as certainly, there was one person in the world who could have prevented it: Michael Atkins. It was an accident. But it was also a crime. And at the end of the trial I'm going to stand up again and ask you to return a verdict of guilty to the charge of manslaughter in the first degree. Thank you."

Brunelle returned to his seat and accepted a tight, professional nod from Yamata, the most a prosecutor will do in such a serious situation. No high fives in front of the jury. It was a good enough opening. It was time to see if Jacobsen could match it.

"Ladies and gentleman of the jury," Judge Quinn announced, "please give your attention to Mr. Jacobsen, who will deliver the opening statement on behalf of the defendant."

CHAPTER 33

Jacobsen took a stance directly in front of the jury box. He was a large man and used his stature to command the room. He clasped his hands in front of him to signal he was about to speak.

"When you hear hoof beats," he said, "don't look for zebras."

Brunelle suppressed a grimace. It was an old lawyers' phrase. All the lawyers knew it. But likely none of the jurors did. So it was effective. That's why it had survived to be an old lawyers' phrase.

"Sometimes the most obvious answer is the correct answer," Jacobsen translated. "And sometimes an accident is just that. An accident. Nothing more."

That time Brunelle suppressed a nod. Jacobsen was right: that was where their battle was joined.

"Let me tell you a little about Michael Atkins," Jacobsen continued. He too looked back at the defendant, but his expression showed warmth. Brunelle knew it was a practiced mask. He also knew the jury didn't know that.

"Michael," Jacobsen said, "lives in Kirkland. He has a condo near the downtown park and likes to watch the sun set over Lake

Washington. He enjoys hiking and kayaking, and he recently took up cycling after he had to stop jogging because of a knee injury. He works for a small software start-up in Kirkland, he likes romantic comedies, and his favorite food is pad thai."

Jacobsen paused and looked to the floor. Dramatic effect. Time for Brunelle to suppress an eye roll.

Jacobsen raised his gaze again, practically biting his lip with faux emotion. "And he loved Tina Belfair with all his heart."

Brunelle usually tried to avoid looking at jurors directly during the defense opening statement. He didn't want to be seen scanning them for reaction, or overly interested in what he, by virtue of his adversarial position, must think is a load of B.S. But he snuck a glance to see if Jacobsen's dramatic ploy had worked. From what Brunelle could gather, it had mixed success. There were definitely a few jurors who seemed engaged, but for every pair of moist eyes, there were a pair of crossed arms elsewhere in the jury box. *Good*, he thought, and returned his eyes to the notepad before him.

"Michael and Tina met about five years ago," Jacobsen continued. "They joined the same hiking club. One day they ended up next to each other on a hike and started talking. They got along and soon enough talking led to flirting. Flirting led to a first date. A first date ended in a first kiss. They became a couple. And then something wonderful happened. Not only were they compatible when it came to hiking and romantic comedies, but they were also compatible sexually." He paused and lowered his voice just enough that it wasn't too creepy. "Very compatible."

He nodded, to let his characterization of their relationship sink in. "In fact, they were more than just compatible, they were complimentary."

Jacobsen paused again. This was where it would have made sense to get into details. But it also would have been uncomfortable.

The jurors needed to be eased into it. They didn't need some middle-aged guy in a suit suddenly talking about bondage.

"You'll hear all the details later," he promised. "What's important to understand now is this: not only did Tina and Michael love each other, but they had something very special. Unique even. And Michael would never, ever have done anything to jeopardize that."

Brunelle couldn't quite suppress a frown. That was a good point. Then again, people screwed up good relationships all the time, because they were too dense to see a good thing when they had it. Everybody knew that.

"So, ladies and gentlemen," Jacobsen began to wrap up, "I'm going to ask you to do one of the hardest things any person can do. I'm going to ask you to keep an open mind. Not just about Michael and Tina's relationship, but about this case. The prosecution gets to go first. They get to put on evidence, and call witnesses, and present their case. All I get to do is cross examine the witnesses they choose to put on. And so it's entirely possible at the end of their case, you'll think Michael is guilty. But remember, you've only heard one side of the story, and the judge has told you and will tell you again and again, you cannot begin deliberating this case until you've heard all of the evidence. And that includes the evidence we put on. You're going to hear from an expert in relationships like Michael and Tina's. He's going to explain to you how perfect they were for each other, and how this case is nothing more than a terrible, tragic accident. And you're going to hear from Michael himself. He's going to tell you how much he loved Tina, how much he misses her, and how he would do anything to have her back."

One more pause. Obviously, Jacobsen was going to emphasize Michael and Tina's Freaky Love throughout the trial. If the leash doesn't fit, you must acquit.

"And then, at the conclusion of this trial," Jacobsen

summarized, "after you've heard all of the evidence, I'm going to stand up again and ask you to find Michael Atkins not guilty. Thank you."

Jacobsen returned to his seat. Judge Quinn waited for him to do so—giving him one extra pause for his words to sink in on the jury—before looking to Brunelle and Yamata.

"The State may call its first witness."

Brunelle stood up. "The State calls Patrick Gillespie."

CHAPTER 34

Patrick Gillespie walked into the courtroom, looking as comfortable as a chicken at a fox convention. His eyes darted around the room, and sweat was already beading his brow before the judge even swore him in. As he sat down in the witness chair, he took a deep breath and exhaled it loudly, like he was about to confess all of his sins, to his wife, with a cop and a stenographer present.

Ordinarily, Brunelle preferred his witnesses to be more at ease, but he supposed it didn't really matter in this case. The jury didn't have to like Gillespie; they just had to believe him.

"Could you state your name for the record?" Brunelle asked from his spot at the back of the jury box. It forced the witness to look toward the jury and keep his voice up. Vital with a civilian witness. Especially a nervous one.

"Uh, Patrick Gillespie," he managed to answer, not without some initial hesitation.

But Brunelle knew the secret to getting a witness comfortable: keep asking them questions, and about things they know. They focus on the information, the memories and the responses, and forget that they're nervous. It just took some of them longer than others. Gillespie looked like he might take a while.

"What do you do for a living, Mr. Gillespie?" Brunelle continued. He moderated his voice into an even, confident cadence, both to offset Gillespie and to encourage him to relax.

"Uh, I own a business," he replied. Witnesses usually spent the first few questions wondering why the stupid lawyer was asking question they already knew the answer to. "A club," he clarified.

Brunelle nodded. "What's the name of the club?"

Gillespie offered a self-conscious grin. "The Cu-CUM-ber Club."

Brunelle supposed the jury probably thought it was a vegan co-op. Nope.

"And what kind of club is it?"

"Uh," Gillespie shifted in his seat and rubbed the back of his neck. His eyes darted toward the jury, then up at the judge. He seemed unsure whether he was allowed to really say what kind of club it was. He was in a courtroom after all. "We have lots of things there. Music, drinks, uh… shows. Events." Another neck rub and glance at the judge. "Education and outreach."

Brunelle appreciated Gillespie's desire to 'keep it clean.' Ordinarily that would be appreciated. But it was a homicide trial. Those are never clean. It was time to get dirty.

"It's a sex club, right?"

That caught the jury's attention. They all looked quickly from Brunelle, the question-asker, to Gillespie, the one who would confirm Brunelle's admittedly leading inquiry.

But he didn't. "Well, no actually." He suddenly seemed much more comfortable. "It's not just a club for people to come and have sex. We have one of the best bars on Capitol Hill, and there's plenty to do besides sex. In the front area, we have pool tables, darts, there's even a room off the main floor with flat-screens to watch sports."

Brunelle frowned. He hadn't really noticed the pool tables and flat-screens when he'd been there. He'd been too busy looking at the dead body on the floor. And the photos on the wall.

But those had been in the back. He needed to lead Gillespie into the back too, and the jury would come along.

"So people can come to your club and just drink and play pool, right?"

Gillespie nodded. "Right."

"But if they want to do more," Brunelle continued, "they can do that too, right? There's a back section, right?'

Gillespie nodded again. "Uh, right. We do have rooms people can rent."

"And the events and shows you mentioned earlier," Brunelle pressed, "those relate to sex, right?"

Gillespie thought for a moment. "Not all of them," he deflected. Then he admitted, "But yes. Most of them, I suppose."

"And the—how did you phrase it?—education and outreach as well?"

Again Gillespie considered his answer. "Some of them."

Brunelle suppressed a frown. This was taking too long. Gillespie had lots of useful information. But titillating sex club or not, the jury was going to get bored with the details of the club's business model. Especially when the details were needlessly vague.

Time to cut to the chase.

"Did any of these events or outreach programs deal with bondage?"

There was a perceptible reaction throughout the courtroom to this first official use of the term 'bondage' in the trial. It would pass, Brunelle knew. By the end of the trial, the jury would probably be as bored with it as they were with everything else in their lives.

Gillespie shrugged. "I'm sure they did. I don't keep real

close track of the subjects. We have several series of classes, led by outside teachers. That's not really my area of expertise. I'm a businessman, and that's one more way to get people in the door."

Brunelle nodded. That was a good enough answer. He could get into the specifics of it later. It was time to get into the heart of the case anyway.

"Did you know Tina Belfair?"

"Yes," Gillespie nodded. "I knew Tina for years. She was one of our regulars."

"How well did you know her?" Brunelle asked.

Gillespie shrugged. "Pretty well. She was a friendly type, so we talked sometimes. I didn't know her that well, I suppose, but I knew she and Michael were a couple. Everybody knew that."

Brunelle nodded. That was fine. It didn't really hurt his case any. And besides, it was true. Move on.

"Were you working the night Tina died?"

Gillespie started to answer, but the reply got stuck in his throat. "Yes," he croaked after a moment.

"And did you see her that night?"

Gillespie nodded, as he recalled. "Yes. I saw her in the main room. I didn't see Michael." Gillespie nodded toward Atkins. "But I knew he was around somewhere. They were always together."

Brunelle frowned internally. One more piece of information that fit the defense narrative better than it fit his. But he could work with it. "Did she seem in good spirits?"

Gillespie thought for a moment. "Yeah." He shrugged. "Sure. Nothing special, but she wasn't down or anything. She seemed to be having a good time."

Brunelle nodded. Small detail but important. She wasn't depressed or suicidal or anything. She didn't have a death wish. Time to move on.

"When was the next time you saw Tina?"

This response didn't just get caught in Gillespie's throat. It choked him and made him tear up. "When she was..." He couldn't bring himself to say it. "When Michael came and got me."

The craft of direct examination was preparing a series of questions and leading the witness logically through the script. The art of direct examination was knowing when to deviate from the script. Brunelle had planned to have Gillespie describe Tina. But he would get back to that.

"Could you describe Mr. Atkins appearance and demeanor when he came and found you?"

It was a natural enough question. The next logical one really, given Gillespie's preceding response. That was why Brunelle had gone off script. Jurors, like everyone else, best understood things they already expected to hear. When answers are anticipated, actual responses become confirmations of already held opinions. People love having their own opinions and expectations validated. To the extent that most people ignore data that doesn't fit their preconceived notions. Being a trial attorney is about convincing people you're right; it's about letting them suspect you're right and confirming it.

"Michael was really upset," Gillespie recalled. "Almost hysterical. He came running into the main room and grabbed me by my shirt and said, 'I think I killed Tina.'"

Another important part of being a trial attorney was paying close attention to the words people used.

"What did he say?" Brunelle asked, even though he'd heard Gillespie response perfectly well. The jury needed to hear it again.

Gillespie squirmed a bit in his seat, obviously uncomfortable at doing anything to hurt his friend's case. But Jacobsen didn't object, so Gillespie had to answer. "He said, 'I think I killed Tina.'"

Gillespie likely didn't fully understand the significance of that statement. The jury likely didn't either. So Brunelle explained it.

"He said, 'I think I killed Tina,'" Brunelle confirmed, "Not 'I think Tina's dead.'?"

Gillespie paused before answering. He looked over to Atkins, as did everyone else in the courtroom, including all the jurors and even Judge Quinn. Then everyone looked back to Gillespie. "Uh, yeah. I think so. I'm not really sure. But something like that."

Brunelle nodded. He figured Gillespie would back away from it. That just proved two things: it hurt Atkins, and it was true.

That would have been a good note to end the direct on, but there was still the issue of Tina's body. It wasn't as compelling, but it was expected, and jurors hold it against the prosecution—as they should, given the burden of proof—if they don't hear the whole story. So quick and dirty with Tina's remains. So to speak.

"Did you see Tina's body that night?"

Gillespie grimaced. "Yes," he recalled, obviously unpleasantly.

"Could you please describe what you saw and what you did?"

The question called for a narrative response—normally objectionable, but Jacobsen didn't seem to be the objecting type. That was nice for just then, but Brunelle hoped he'd end up being more unreasonable later in the trial. The one time the jury doesn't hold it against the prosecutor if they don't hear the whole story, is when they don't hear it because the defense attorney objected.

"Well, the first thing I did is ask Michael what happened. Again, he said he thought he'd killed Tina, or she was dead, or something like that. I said, show me where she is, and we went back to one of the private rooms. She was in there, on the floor, not moving. She had a lot of restraints on—rope mostly. I knew Michael had panicked because he hadn't even cut the ropes off. I checked for a pulse but it was pretty obvious she was dead."

"So what did you do?"

"I backed out of there and took Michael to my office. I told one of the waiters to not let anybody in the room, then I called 911."

Good enough. Brunelle nodded to his witness. "Thank you, Mr. Gillespie. I have no further questions."

Brunelle returned to his seat next to Yamata and Judge Quinn looked to Jacobsen. "Any cross examination?" she asked.

Jacobsen stood up and straightened his suit coat. "Just briefly. Thank you, Your Honor."

The defense attorney stepped around his counsel table and approached the witness.

"You knew Michael and Tina for several years, correct?" he started.

Gillespie was eager to agree. "Oh, yes."

"And they were a happy couple, isn't that right?"

Again, quick agreement. "Absolutely."

"In fact, they were devoted to each other, isn't that true?"

Brunelle noted that Jacobsen was doing a good job of leading the witness, the core of cross examination. Don't ask the witness for an answer. Give him the answer and make him agree with you. Which, it turned out, Gillespie was more than happy to do.

"Yes," Gillespie answered dutifully. "They were devoted to each other."

"Michael would never have hurt Tina, correct?"

But Gillespie hesitated. "Uh..."

"I mean," Jacobsen interjected, "without Tina's consent."

Gillespie accepted that caveat. "Right. Never without her consent. They had a very good understanding of each other."

Jacobsen nodded. He'd gotten what he needed. That's when the better defense attorneys sit down. "No further questions, Your

Honor."

Brunelle suppressed yet another frown. Jacobsen was proving himself to be one of the better defense attorneys.

"Any redirect?" Quinn asked Brunelle.

Brunelle stood up to answer. "No, Your Honor."

"You may be excused," the judge told the witness, and Gillespie was only too glad to hurry off the witness stand and toward the door.

Quinn looked to Brunelle. "You may call your next witness."

"Thank you, Your Honor," Brunelle replied. "The State calls Detective Larry Chen."

CHAPTER 35

Chen walked through the court room doors and straight to the witness stand. He knew the drill.

Brunelle stood up and took his place at the bar. He knew the drill too. "Please state your name for the record."

"Lawrence Chen."

"How are you employed sir?"

"I'm a detective with the Seattle Police Department."

"How long have you been with the Seattle Police Department?"

"I've been a cop for over twenty years."

It was the same question-and-answer dance they'd done dozens of times before. Each knew what the other would say next. Brunelle had Chen's qualifications memorized. But the jury had just met him, so they had to go through the whole bit. Once more, from the top!

"How long have you been a detective?"

"I've been a detective going on eight years now."

"Are you assigned to any particular department or division?"

"I'm assigned to the Homicide Division."

"And what are your duties as a detective in the homicide division?"

"I respond to reports of suspicious deaths and other major crimes."

Okay, enough orienting the jury. Time to get to it.

"Do you remember responding to a report of a suspicious death at the Cu-CUM-ber Club on Twelfth Avenue on Seattle's Capitol Hill?"

Until then, Chen had been delivering his answers back to Brunelle. But now his answers mattered. He turned to the jury to tell them, "Yes, I did."

"And was the deceased eventually identified as Christina Belfair?"

Chen frowned slightly. Just the right amount to show he'd seen a lot in his career, but he still cared despite it. "Yes."

Brunelle nodded and paused. Approximating respect for the dead. Then move on. "Please describe the scene when you first arrived."

Chen returned the nod, then turned to the jury again. "When I arrived, there were already other units on scene. The first officers who responded to the original call. I don't get called out until a patrol officer determines a detective is needed. By the time I got there, the scene was locked down, but there were very few patrons left, and the ones who were, didn't know anything. Or at least that's what they said." Chen offered a lopsided smile. "Those are usually the only people willing to stay and wait for the cops."

Some of the jurors nodded or chuckled slightly at that observation. *Good*, thought Brunelle, *they liked him*. Everybody liked Larry Chen.

"So what did you do next?" Brunelle asked. He was required by the evidence rules to interrupt a witness' testimony with the occasional question, lest the witness go too far off course or say something they shouldn't. But Chen was a professional, so Jacobsen was unlikely to interrupt with an objection, or have any cause to.

"I located the manager," Chen answered, "a Mr. Gillespie. He led me back to the room where the body—where *Christina* was."

Good catch, Brunelle thought. Make sure the jury remembers there was a real live person before the defendant killed her. That sometimes got lost in a trial focused on the defendant's rights, and where the murder victim, by definition, can't testify.

"Did you inspect the body at all?" Brunelle asked. It didn't hurt to also remind the jury that Christina had turned into 'a body.'

Chen shook his head. "Not closely. She was clearly deceased. The EMTs had already discontinued revival efforts. We were just waiting for the M.E.—the medical examiner—to show up. So we locked down the room and Mr. Gillespie took me to his office to speak with Mr. Atkins." Chen turned and nodded toward the defense table. "The defendant."

Another good thing to remind the jury of.

Brunelle nodded. This was where Chen's testimony was the most valuable. Not his own words, but introducing the defendant's words.

"Did Mr. Atkins agree to speak with you?"

"Yes."

"And did you advise him of his constitutional rights before asking him any questions?"

Chen turned to the jurors for this response. It was for them anyway. If the answer had been 'no' the judge never would have allowed any testimony about it in the first place. "Yes," he answered.

"What did Mr. Atkins say happened?"

Chen looked down for a moment in thought, then looked up to the jurors. "Yes. He said he killed her."

Brunelle smiled inside. If only he could have sat down after that answer, he would have. But Jacobsen was going to get to ask questions next, so he needed to explain a bit more. Be honest with the jury. And candid.

"Was he more specific than that?" Brunelle asked.

"A little bit," Chen confirmed.

"What did he say specifically?"

Chen thought for a moment then turned again to the jury. "He said they were playing a bondage game. He tied her up so she couldn't really move. Eventually he noticed she was unconscious. He tried to wake her up, but when it appeared she wasn't breathing, he panicked and ran for help."

Brunelle nodded solemnly. Honesty didn't require a complete lack of theater. He knew the answer to his next, and last, question. A small pause, just beyond the question-and-answer tempo he and Chen had established, would ensure the attention of all the jurors. "What was the last thing Mr. Atkins said?"

Chen knew that would be Brunelle's last question. Not because they'd rehearsed it. Because they knew each other. And because it had to be his final answer.

"The last thing he said," Chen explained, "was, 'Tina's dead, and it's all my fault.'"

Brunelle nodded one last time. "No further questions."

As he returned to his seat and flashed Jacobsen the briefest of challenging glances. 'Follow that,' it said. Jacobsen stood up and returned his own look. 'Oh, I will.'

Jacobsen stood up and strode casually to his own spot at the bar. It was two steps closer than Brunelle. Still a respectful distance, but more aggressive. To communicate that he was hostile, because his demeanor was smooth as silk.

"Mr. Atkins was cooperative, wasn't he, Detective Chen?"

Chen thought for a moment, then nodded. "Yes." He'd testified enough to know short answers were the best answers on cross.

"He was honest, correct?" Jacobsen continued. "And candid, right?"

Chen also knew when not to agree. "He answered my questions. I can't say how honest he was. Most people lie to me, at least a little."

Jacobsen surrendered a tight frown. But he wasn't one to be pushed off course by a witness. "He didn't hold back though, correct? He answered every one of your questions, right?"

Chen paused. But he had to admit, "Yes, that's true."

"And what it all boiled down to is that this was all just a horrible accident, isn't that correct?"

Brunelle knew he could probably object. It was speculation, and it was an opinion on the ultimate issue. The types of objections you learn in law school. The type of objections that get overruled. He'd just have to rely on Chen. And he knew he could.

"Accident?" Chen repeated. "No, this was no accident. The word 'accident' suggests something unavoidable. This wasn't an accident. This was a mistake."

Jacobsen's expression hardened. But he couldn't sit down on that answer. He had to salvage something. "So it wasn't intentional, correct?"

Chen surrendered his own expression. A begrudging smile. "Correct."

Jacobsen sat down. He'd scored what points he could, and he couldn't trick Chen.

Brunelle stood up. He had one more point and he could trust Chen.

"It wasn't intentional?" Brunelle confirmed. "But it was reckless, wasn't it?"

Jacobsen could have objected too. For all the same reasons, plus it was leading. But the judge would have overruled those too.

He sat and waited for the answer just like everybody else.

"Yes," Chen was visibly pleased to answer. "It was reckless."

And there were no further questions for the lead detective.

CHAPTER 36

After Chen came a series of secondary witnesses. Patrons who'd seen Tina and Michael earlier that night. Patrol officers who locked down the scene. Forensic officers who took photographs and collected evidence. Not terribly interesting, but necessary to complete the story. Because an incomplete story could lead to doubts, and doubts lead to acquittals.

It was important to finish strong, though, and so special consideration needed to be given to the final witness. In an assault case, you start with the victim and finish with the doctor. In a homicide case, the victim can't testify, so it was all the more important to finish with the medical examiner.

"The State calls Dr. Kat Anderson." It was a phrase Brunelle had said a dozen times. But this time it was Yamata who called the M.E. to the stand.

Brunelle was going to avoid looking at Kat as she walked through the doors to the courtroom and realized he wasn't going to be doing her direct examination. But he stole a glance despite himself. The initial surprise and confusion on her countenance were quickly pushed aside by realization and irritation. And disappointment. Which was why he hadn't wanted to look in the first place.

He lowered his head over his legal pad and pretended to take notes while Yamata handled the strong finish.

"Please state your name for the record," Yamata's voice began confidently.

"Kat Anderson," came the reply. Brunelle still didn't look up. He imagined Kat was staring at him. But he knew she wasn't. Which bothered him even more.

"How are you employed?"

"I'm an assistant medical examiner with the King County Medical Examiner's Office."

Then came her degrees and training, her qualifications and experience. Brunelle knew them by heart. She was a very impressive woman. A very impressive person.

"Do your duties," Yamata inquired, "include responding to the scenes of suspicious deaths and conducting autopsies?"

"Yes." A simple, elegant syllable. Brunelle dared a glance. Kat's eyes were fixed squarely on her questioner. Yamata. He knew it should have been him. He returned his eyes to the doodles on his yellow pad.

"Did you respond to a report of a suspicious death at the Cu-CUM-Ber Club in Seattle?"

"Yes."

How could she make that one syllable so sensual?

"Please tell the jury what you encountered."

Another stolen glimpse and Brunelle caught Kat's perfect profile as she looked to the jury and explained, "I encountered a female subject who had died prior to my arrival."

"What was the condition of the body?"

"She had died within the preceding hour, so the body was still warm to the touch and rigor had not yet set in."

A doctor's answer. Brunelle smiled slightly. He knew that

wasn't what the lawyer wanted.

"Let me be more specific," Yamata said. "How was she dressed and was there anything of note, uh, attached to her body?"

"Ah," Kat replied. Another perfectly formed syllable. "The body was partially dressed in a leather costume. Her arms and legs were bound with rope."

"Did you observe any injuries on the body?"

A pause, then, "Not at the scene. However, at autopsy, I did observe several bruises at various stages of healing on her back and legs. Speaking with law enforcement later, it appears those bruises were not related to the death." Another pause. "Well, not directly anyway."

"So you conducted an autopsy?"

"Yes. We almost always conduct autopsies for unnatural deaths. And certainly when the death is the subject of a criminal investigation."

"Were you able to determine a cause or manner of death?"

"I was able to determine both a cause and a manner of death."

"What's the difference?"

Brunelle knew Yamata knew, but he also knew Yamata knew the jury didn't know.

"Cause of death," Kat explained, "means the specific mechanism that caused the person to die. A gunshot wound, for example. Manner of death refers to one of four statutory categories that all deaths fall into: homicide, suicide, accident, and natural causes."

"What was the cause of Tina Belfair's death?"

"The cause of death was hypoxia."

"And what is hypoxia?"

Another quick glance. Kat was in full professor mode, punctuating her explanation with graceful hand gestures. He loved how she moved.

"Hypoxia is a condition when there is inadequate oxygen in the blood and tissue, which can be, and in this case was, fatal."

"What's the difference between hypoxia and strangulation or suffocation?"

"One way to think of it, is that strangulation or suffocation lead to hypoxia. Hypoxia means you don't have enough oxygen. Being strangled or suffocated will certainly do that, but there are other ways."

"What other ways?"

"It can occur during activities like mountain climbing, when there isn't enough oxygen in the air to begin with."

"So was Tina strangled to death?"

A logical conclusion, Brunelle knew. But also incorrect. But Kat would explain it. She always knew what was really going on.

"No. Strangulation will leave behind several telltale signs, including obvious signs like broken blood vessels in the eyes— something called petechiae. That wasn't present here. Although there was some squeezing of the flesh, which led to the blanching, there was no indication that her airways or arteries were constricted."

This time it was Yamata who paused. Strategically, to ensure the jury's attention, and mimic their own likely uncertainty. "So what happened?" she asked.

"The hypoxia was caused by a substantially reduced intake of air over an extended period of time. She could still breathe, but not deeply. Our bodies periodically need to take deep breaths, expanding our rib cages to do it. If the rib cage is prevented from opening wide enough, and especially if the mouth or nose is also partially blocked, the body simply can't take in enough air, and a person can die of hypoxia even though they can still breath somewhat."

Another pause. Brunelle looked up to see if she knew enough to move on. He looked down again because he knew she did. And because Kat started to peer over at him.

"Did you say you determined a manner of death?" Yamata asked, to signal the change in topic and orient the jury on the impending answer.

"Yes."

"And what was that determination based on?"

"It was based on the cause of death and the condition of the body upon initial examination at the scene."

"Did it appear that another person had contributed to the cause of death?"

"Yes."

"So what was the manner of death?"

Brunelle didn't have to look up to know Kat turned to the jury to deliver what would be her final answer on direct exam. "Homicide."

"No further questions," Yamata announced and she took her seat next to Brunelle. He tried to offer a 'good job', but his co-counsel was focused squarely on the defense attorney as he stood up to begin his cross examination.

"Homicide, you say?" Jacobsen began, his voice almost folksy. Brunelle again focused on the words without looking at the witness. He knew Kat could take care of herself.

"Yes. Homicide."

"But homicide doesn't mean murder, right? Or even manslaughter?"

"Murder and manslaughter are legal terms," Kat admitted. "Those terms describe when a homicide is also a crime. I don't determine that. The jury does."

"Exactly," Jacobsen replied. "Now what's the difference between homicide and an accident? If I crash my car and kill someone, is that homicide or an accident?"

Kat paused as she considered the question. "If you intended to crash your car and injure someone, then it would be homicide. If you crashed for other reasons and someone ended up dying, that would probably be an accident."

"So are you saying my client intended to kill his girlfriend?"

Kat knew not to take the bait. But the honest answer wasn't going to help Brunelle any. He wondered absently whether she even cared about that any more. "No," she answered. "I'm not saying that."

"So, really, the manner of death was accident?"

Kat hesitated. "I still believe it was homicide. The mechanism of death—the restraints—were placed on her intentionally."

"But never with the intent that she die."

"If you say so," Kat tried.

But Jacobsen wasn't going to just accept that type of reply. "I don't say so, doctor. You do. You said if a person causes a death, but didn't mean to, that's an accident."

"I said," Kat's voice hardened, "that if a person dies as a result of another person's intentional act, that's homicide."

A long pause as Jacobsen obviously considered whether to continue the battle. He wisely chose against it. He'd made his point and could return to it in his closing argument. So instead he circled back to his main point. "Homicide, but not manslaughter, correct?"

"It was homicide," Kat replied. "I can't say more than that."

"I bet you could," Jacobsen needled, "but you've said enough for me. Thank you, doctor."

He returned to his seat and confirmed, "No further questions, Your Honor."

Quinn looked to Yamata. "Any redirect examination, counsel?"

Yamata thought for a moment then stood up. "Tina Belfair wouldn't have died that night but for the restraints placed on her by the defendant, correct?"

Kat thought for a moment. "I think that's fair to say."

"No further questions." And Yamata sat down.

Quinn looked back to Jacobsen. "Re-cross?"

Jacobsen stood as if to ask another question, but then grinned. "No, Your Honor. The defense is satisfied with the good doctor's testimony. Thank you."

Brunelle shook his head ever so slightly, and looked at his final doodle: the word 'JACKASS'—but the squiggly arrow that accompanied the letters was pointed directly at himself.

CHAPTER 37

After Kat had walked out of the courtroom--possibly glaring at Brunelle, but he didn't know for sure because he still wasn't looking at her--Brunelle stood up and importantly announced, "The State rests."

The good news was, they were done with their case. They had presented the best evidence they had in the best possible way, and now they could relax, just a little, and prepare for whatever evidence the defense might choose to put on.

The bad news was, the judge adjourned early for the day and Kat was still in the building. She was waiting outside his office when he stepped off the elevator.

"What the hell was that?" she demanded. She shoved a fist on a perfectly curved hip as she said it. Brunelle really liked her hips.

But he could keep his wits about him.

"What the hell was what?" He taught his witnesses, if they needed a little extra time to think about an answer, they should ask the attorney to rephrase the question. He just did the normal conversation equivalent.

"You had Yamata do the questioning?" Kat sneered.

Brunelle tried to shrug casually. "I thought she could use the experience."

Kat narrowed her eyes. "She's plenty experienced, David."

Brunelle raised an eyebrow and considered her comment. "Is that some kind of sex thing? Are you suggesting there's something going on between me and Yamata?"

Guilty consciences speak loudly.

But Kat laughed, rather scornfully in fact. "No, I wasn't suggesting that at all. But maybe I should have. You've been M.I.A. for weeks now. I practically forgot what you looked like."

Brunelle shrugged and looked away. "It's this case. You know how I get when I'm in trial."

"Bullshit," Kat barked. Brunelle's gaze snapped back to her hardened face. "You get distracted, distant even, but nothing like this. And this case brought us closer at the beginning. You were all over me, literally."

Brunelle felt his mouth tip into a weak smile, but he didn't say anything.

Kat's expression softened ever so slightly. "What's going on, David?"

Another shrug, another look away. "Nothing."

But Kat wouldn't have it. "Don't lie to me, David. It's me. It's Kat. You can be honest with me."

Brunelle smiled again, ruefully this time. Honesty. And candor. He could give her honesty, but not candor.

Honesty: "This case has led to a lot of things that are distracting me."

Candor: *And I'm fucking her.*

He shook his head and walked past her to his office. "I'm sorry, Kat."

And that was true too.

CHAPTER 38

The biggest mystery of a criminal trial was whether a defendant would testify. The second biggest mystery was, if he did, then when. The prosecution can't force a defendant to testify, or even call him as a witness and force him to assert his right to remain silent. And the one thing the prosecution can never do is make any comment on what a defendant might or might not say until he actually does. And if he doesn't, then the prosecutor can't say anything at all. The defense holds all those cards, and doesn't have to play them until after the State rests its case. So the next morning, Brunelle had to be prepared for Master Michael taking the stand, but also for any other defense witness. And if it ended up being someone other than the defendant, then Brunelle would have to conduct his cross exam not knowing whether or not Atkins might eventually take the stand after all. That was far more difficult than if Atkins testified first. Jacobsen knew that, of course. And so, of course, Jacobsen's first witness was Dr. Peter Sylvan, Sexologist.

The only good news was that Robyn had come to watch the trial again. Interest in the subject matter, Brunelle knew. Oh, how he knew. Cross exam was going to be hard enough without being distracted by his memories of Robyn, each a potential illustration for Sylvan's next book.

Sylvan practically threw the doors open and all heads turned as he marched importantly to the witness stand. He clearly enjoyed being watched. A different topic for a different cross examination, Brunelle supposed.

The judge swore Sylvan in and Jacobsen proceeded with the same introduction he'd done at the motion to dismiss. Sylvan introduced himself, listed his degrees, explained what sexology was, and again described his area of focus as 'nonreciprocal power relationships coupled with device and restraint protocols.'

That got everyone's attention.

"Are you familiar with the case of Michael Atkins and Christina Belfair?" Jacobsen asked.

Brunelle had to hand it to Jacobsen. That was a good way to put it. It wasn't State vs. Atkins, homicide. It was Michael and Tina, true love.

"Yes," Sylvan confirmed.

"And how are you familiar with it?"

This time, Sylvan turned to the jury to explain, "I have reviewed all of the police reports, as well as related documentation such as the autopsy report. I also met with Mr. Atkins multiple times to discuss the case. In addition, I am quite familiar with the location of Tina's death, the Cu-CUM-Ber Club." Then he turned ever so slightly back and Brunelle swore Sylvan glanced out of the corner of his eye at him to add, "And other similar clubs, such as The Opal Room and others."

And Brunelle was rattled, despite himself.

"So, doctor," Jacobsen asked, "do you have an opinion as to the manner of Tina Belfair's death?"

"Yes," Sylvan answered simply. He'd testified before and undoubtedly rehearsed with Jacobsen. He knew he'd get to state his opinion in a few more questions.

"And what was that opinion based on?"

Sylvan again looked to the jury. It was important to the defense that they knew why they should trust his opinion. "It was based on my review of the aforementioned reports, my interviews with Mr. Atkins, my interviews with friends and family of both Michael and Tina, as well as my own experience and training in the area of sexology."

"What conclusions did you draw about Michael and Tina's relationship?" Jacobsen started with.

"Michael and Tina were in a long-term monogamous relationship," Sylvan replied. "Sexually, they enjoyed a dominant-submissive dynamic where Michael was the dominant partner and Tina was the submissive. These roles were apparently never reversed, even in play. Each derived sexual satisfaction from the dynamic, which they augmented with restraint play and the use of sexual aids."

"And what conclusions did you draw," Jacobsen continued, "about their activities the night Tina died?"

"Their activities that night were entirely consensual," Sylvan said. "The dominant-submissive dynamic does not imply any lack of consent on the part of the submissive partner. To the contrary, the entire point is that the submissive is consenting to the power of the dominant."

And the pay-off question. "What conclusion did you draw regarding the manner of Christina Belfair's death?"

With its pay-off answer. "Tina's death was an accident." Then, just in case the jury didn't get it, and before Brunelle could object for giving an opinion on the ultimate issue, Sylvan added, "It wasn't manslaughter."

Brunelle felt the rush of the word 'Objection!' under his skin, but it was too late, and he didn't want to draw any more attention to that last sentence of Sylvan's. All the judge could do was instruct the jury to disregard it, which would ensure that they didn't. You can't, as the lawyers say, un-ring a bell.

So instead he waited for Jacobsen to confirm, "No more questions," then stood up and began his cross examination.

He had three goals, the same three goals he had with any expert. Usually it was some retired crime lab guy who'd decided to make a few bucks on the side criticizing his former colleagues' work for a few hundred bucks, or a Ph.D. with book smarts and no practical experience. Sylvan was neither of those, Brunelle knew, but the strategy was the same: attack the discipline, attack the qualifications, attack the conclusion.

"Sexology, huh?" Brunelle started. "That almost sounds made up."

Sylvan was a good witness. He didn't take the bait. Instead, he acknowledged the truth. "I'm afraid you're right. It does. But I assure you, it is an actual discipline and I actually have a Ph.D. in it."

No, not just a good witness. A very good witness. He took Brunelle's barb and used it to remind the jury of his qualifications.

Which Brunelle then clumsily tried to attack. "But a Ph.D. in a made up discipline doesn't seem to be that impressive of an achievement."

Sylvan paused for a moment. "Well, I suppose it wouldn't be, but again, it's a very real and very important discipline. People across the country and across the world benefit greatly from the advances in understanding human sexuality brought about by the scientific study of something which has been a core aspect of who we all are, but until recently was treated as something to be ignored or condemned."

Brunelle frowned. This wasn't going well. He considered attacking Sylvan's personal accomplishments, but decided against giving him another opportunity to recite his degrees and publications.

He glanced around the courtroom. He didn't care about Yamata or Jacobsen or even Master Michael. He just wanted to confirm Robyn was still there. She was. And he was doing a shitty job, right in front of her.

"Uh," he stammered, realizing he was taking too long to ask his next question. "You said Ms. Belfair's death was an accident, not manslaughter. Do you even know the legal definition of manslaughter?"

He could actually hear Robyn's exasperated huff as she stood up and walked out. Brunelle tried to pretend that didn't hurt. He took solace in the fact that she wouldn't see the end of the train wreck his cross had turned into.

"Why, yes," Sylvan replied. Of course. "I am familiar with the definitions of both first degree and second degree manslaughter."

Well, the die was cast, Brunelle realized. He had to follow through now. But that meant not only did Sylvan get to tell the jury that Tina's death wasn't manslaughter, Brunelle was about to give him the chance to explain why.

So he thanked God when the fire alarm went off.

"Oh, Good Lord," Quinn let out. Brunelle agreed. Then the judge regained herself and took control of the situation.

"Counsel and members of the public, please exit the courtroom by way of the main doors. Jurors, please go with my judicial assistant, who keep you together and separate from the public during this fire alarm. We will reconvene in the court room as soon as the fire department gives the all clear to re-enter the building."

Everyone did as they were told. Brunelle hoped the fire department would take their sweet time, maybe even shut the whole building down for the day like they did when that box of spare parts on the loading dock was mistaken for a bomb. But in less than thirty minutes, the public was filing back into the courthouse and Brunelle was going to have to go back in and try to salvage his cross examination. It wasn't even 10:30 yet.

The only bright spot was that, in the confusion of mass reentry he had a moment with Robyn who had emerged from the crowd to confront him in the hallway outside Quinn's courtroom.

"That was horrible," she started. "Just terrible."

Brunelle pasted on a smile. "Why, thank you," he said sarcastically. But he knew she was right.

"You can thank me later," she said enigmatically.

Brunelle's eyebrows knitted together. "For what?"

Robyn rolled her eyes. "I pulled the fire alarm. It was your only hope."

Brunelle was speechless. Robyn often had that effect on him. But this was different. "You..." he started.

"Pulled the fire alarm," she finished. "Yes. You had to be stopped. You don't get it at all. You're going to lose this case."

Brunelle's confusion deepened. Why would she care about that? She was a defense attorney. Didn't she want Jacobsen to win?

But he didn't voice those thoughts, and Robyn stuck with hers. "You need to adjourn for the day. While Sylvan is still on the stand. You need to start your cross all over. You need to figure out the right way to do it." She paused again. "You need me."

Brunelle could hardly argue the last point. "But it's only ten-thirty. Quinn will never let me adjourn for the day. Especially not in the middle of cross examination."

Robyn locked her eyes on Brunelle's. "Tell her your stomach hurts."

But Brunelle shook his head incredulously. "I can't lie to the judge."

Robyn must have agreed, because she punched him square

in the gut. Hard.

Brunelle doubled over, spitting for air. He hadn't expected it at all. Especially not with her eyes locked on his. "What the fuck are you doing?"

"Do you trust me?" Robyn demanded.

Brunelle took a moment to consider the question. She'd just sucker-punched him in the stomach. But he knew the answer. They both did. "Yes."

"Then go in there," Robyn commanded, "and tell her you can't go on any more today. Insist. Make yourself puke if you have to. Get the case adjourned until tomorrow and don't agree to finish your cross first. You need to finish your cross tomorrow."

Brunelle finally managed to stand up straight again, but his stomach still hurt. "Why tomorrow?"

"Because," Robyn grabbed his shirt roughly, "you're going to spend tonight with me."

CHAPTER 39

The ruse worked, although it wasn't truly a ruse. Brunelle didn't lie. Instead, he did that old lawyer trick where each of the sentences was true by itself, but together they misled the listener into a false conclusion.

He told the judge his stomach hurt, which was true. Robyn had punched him pretty hard.

He told the judge that he was having trouble focusing on the case. He was focusing on seeing Robyn that night.

And he told the judge he didn't think his cross examination was very effective. That was obvious to anyone in the courtroom.

But it worked. Judge Quinn, after initial reluctance and with more than a little consternation, gave Brunelle the rest of the day off.

Jacobsen was pissed.

Sylvan seemed amused.

And Brunelle spent the rest of the day in his apartment, completely distracted by thoughts—both memories and fantasies-- of Robyn Dunn.

By the time eight o'clock rolled around, he had worked himself up into quite a fever. As he knocked on Robyn's apartment door, he wasn't sure if he'd be able to keep his cool. But Robyn was. She opened the door and stepped outside before he even got the chance to try to push his way in.

"Not yet, Dave," she chided, as she swiftly locked the door behind her. "We have a long night ahead of us, but it's still a bit early for what I have planned. Let's get a drink. Or two. Then we'll be in the right frame of mind."

Two drinks turned into three. Maybe four. Somewhere in there, Robyn started rubbing his leg. By the time they finally got back to her apartment, Brunelle was ready to pop.

So of course, she wanted to talk.

She pointed at the couch. "Sit down, Dave."

He hesitated. He wanted to go to her bedroom, not the couch. They could fuck on the couch too—he knew that—but there was something in her tone of voice that said he might as well keep his pants buttoned.

He sat down, a bit reluctantly, and clasped his hands between his knees. He was glad for the sitting though; his head was swimming a bit from the alcohol. Robyn stepped into her bedroom for a moment and came back far too quickly, still dressed and holding a paper in her hand. Brunelle wondered if it was some sort of contract or waiver of something. He'd heard that sometimes BDSM couples use contracts. Or was that only the professional dominatrixes? If a prenup sucked the romance out of a marriage, what did a hold-harmless clause do to sexual attraction?

Mercifully, Robyn sat down next to him and interrupted his thoughts. She kept her paper rolled up in her hands.

"What did you think we were going to do tonight?" she asked him.

He thought for a moment, then decided to be honest. "I thought we were going to fuck." Then, after a moment, "Er, have sex."

Robyn laughed. "Just don't say 'make love' or I'll kick you out right now."

Brunelle managed a laugh. And filed the information away. He really liked her.

"What kind of sex did you think he were going to have?" she continued.

Again, a moment to think. "Heterosexual?" He wasn't sure where she was headed with all this, so he defaulted to humor to cover his unease.

She laughed. "Obviously. Anything more than that?"

Brunelle shrugged, like he'd been caught doing something wrong. "Nonreciprocal power sex coupled with device and restraint protocols?" Again, a little humor to cover his true feelings.

Robyn didn't laugh that time, but she smiled. It made her one dimple appear. He really liked that dimple.

"And who did you think would have the greater power in that nonreciprocal relationship?" she asked, peering at him out of the corner of lowered eyes.

"Me?" he hoped aloud.

Robyn's smile stayed static. "Uh-huh. So, we've talked, and we've fucked, and we've played. Do you think you know what I like?'

Brunelle narrowed his eyes in concentration. This wasn't what he'd been expecting. It felt like a job interview. "I think so."

"Do you think you can give me what I need?" she pressed.

He thought for a moment, then nodded. "Yeah. I think I can." Then he considered his word choice, always important when talking with a lawyer. "Yes, I can."

She unrolled the paper and handed it to him. "Read this."

He looked at the piece of paper. At the top, it was titled, 'The Master's Creed.' At the bottom, the footer told him she'd printed it off the internet that afternoon. It read:

Above all else the Dominant cherishes his Submissive, in the knowledge that the gift the Submissive gives him is the greatest gift of all. The Dominant is demanding and takes full advantage of the power given to him, but knows how to share the pleasure that comes from that precious gift.

To win his Submissive's mind, body, spirit, soul, and love, He knows he must first win her trust. He will show his Submissive humor, kindness, and warmth. He must always show her that his guidance and tutoring is knowledgeable and deserving of her attention, that this is a man she can learn from, and trust his direction.

When it comes time to teach his Submissive her lessons, he is a strong and unyielding teacher. He will accept no flaw, nothing less than perfection from his student. Never does he use discipline without a good reason. When he does it is always with a knowledgeable and careful hand.

He is patient, taking time to learn her limits, and knowing that as her trust of him grows, so will they. She responds to him out of the want of pleasing him. Compliance comes from the wanting to please, not the fear of punishment. He understands the fragile nature of mind and body and never violates the trust given to him.

His tools are mind, body, spirit, soul, and love. He understands that each partner gains most from pleasuring the other. And both of them know that love and trust are the only bindings that truly hold.

Brunelle lowered the paper again and looked into Robyn's eyes. But it was she who spoke.

"Dave, you do every fucking thing I tell you." She laughed slightly. It was warm, not in the least mocking, but it stung nonetheless. "You sit when I tell you to sit. You came over tonight fully intent on fucking me as soon as you got here, but I made you go out for two hours and have drinks first—and you did it. Hell, this morning, you quit in the middle of your trial day just because I told you to."

Brunelle lowered his eyes to the floor.

She tapped the paper. "You don't even really understand this kind of relationship, do you?"

He considered lying for a moment, but then, admitted, "No."

"Do you know who does?" she asked.

He thought for a moment and looked up at her. "You?"

She smiled, but avoided the question. "Sylvan. Read this. Try to understand it. Then use Sylvan to hold that bastard responsible for what he did to his sub."

Brunelle looked at The Master's Creed again. He supposed Sylvan was probably familiar with it. He could try to cross him with it. The gears in his head started turning, but Robyn stopped them.

She took his hand. Hers was soft and warm. "There'll be time tomorrow. We can talk more in the morning." She stood up, still holding his hand and took a step toward the bedroom. "Come on, let's make love."

Brunelle allowed himself to be pulled to his feet. "Whatever you say."

CHAPTER 40

The next morning found Brunelle back in Quinn's courtroom, Robyn in the gallery, Sylvan on the stand, and Jacobsen looking uneasy. The defense attorney was enough of a gamesman to suspect Brunelle was up to something with his not-quite-fake stomach pain.

The third biggest mystery in a criminal case was whether the prosecutor could influence the defendant's decision to testify. Generally, it was better if they didn't. Juries are instructed over and over again that a defendant doesn't have to testify and the fact that a defendant has not testified can't be used against him in any way. The reason they're instructed that *ad nauseum* is because it's counter to everything else people do in their lives. If you accuse a child or employee of doing something wrong and they don't deny it, you know they did it. So juries are told not to do something they do all the time and then they trick themselves into believing they didn't do it, all the time thinking in the back of their heads, *If it were me, I would have taken the stand and said I didn't do it.*

It was even worse in this case, where Atkins was reasonably articulate and had a strong emotional appeal to his defense. Manslaughter, accident, or whatever, he had in fact lost his longtime girlfriend. He was going to cry and the tears would likely be real. Another thing jurors are instructed is that they can't let sympathy influence their verdict. Again, because that's exactly what they'll do.

So when Brunelle resumed his cross examination, his goal wasn't just to get Sylvan to agree with him, it was to scare Atkins into changing his mind and not taking the stand.

"You testified yesterday," Brunelle began, "that you believe Tina's death was an accident, not manslaughter. Is that right?"

Sylvan nodded confidently. "That's correct."

"You also said you familiarized yourself with the manslaughter statute in order to be able to render that opinion, correct?"

Another nod, but a bit less confident. Sylvan knew Brunelle was the expert on the law, and he knew Brunelle was going somewhere with the questioning, even if he wasn't sure where yet. "I did read the statute, yes."

"Manslaughter means recklessly killing someone, right?" Brunelle asked.

The entire line of questioning normally would have been objectionable. Witnesses weren't supposed to do the legal analysis—that was the jury's job. But Jacobsen had opened the door, and both lawyers knew it. Jacobsen sat objectionless and Brunelle pressed forward.

"That sounds correct," Sylvan conceded.

"And reckless means two things. First, that you knew of a risk and disregarded it, and second, that disregarding the risk was a gross deviation from that of a reasonable person, correct?"

Sylvan frowned slightly. "I do recall that."

"That's what we lawyers call a reasonable person standard," Brunelle said.

"Okay," Sylvan replied to the non-question.

"But didn't you testify that the type of relationship Tina and Michael had was unusual?"

Sylvan took the bait. "I didn't say 'unusual. I said uncommon. Not everyone understands the bond those two enjoyed." He thought for a moment, then added, "So to speak."

Under different circumstances, that might have been funny, but Brunelle was focused and serious and the rest of the courtroom was mirroring his demeanor.

"Uncommon," Brunelle repeated back. "So should Mr. Atkins be judged according to the way everyone thinks, or should his actions be judged by the standards of those who understand his and Tina's uncommon bond?"

Easy answer for Sylvan. Too easy, he should have realized. "Mr. Atkins actions should only be judged within the context, and with a full understanding of, his special relationship with Ms. Belfair."

Thank you, Brunelle thought.

His next actions were done slowly and in silence, to draw everyone's attention to them. He stepped back to his counsel table. He pulled two pieces of paper out of a manila folder he'd set atop his legal pad before starting his questions. He walked over to the clerk and had one copy marked as an exhibit. He stepped back over and handed the unmarked copy to Jacobsen. Then he handed the marked exhibit to Sylvan.

"Are you familiar," Brunelle asked the sexologist, "with something known as The Master's Creed?"

"Objection." Jacobsen stood up. He tried to look casual, bored almost. Perturbed certainly. He didn't want the jury to know how much this might hurt his case.

Brunelle waited a beat, then looked up to the judge. "The basis for the objection?"

Judge Quinn looked to Jacobsen. "What's your basis,

counsel?"

"Mr. Brunelle is trying to confuse the jury, Your Honor," Jacobsen replied. "He's produced some made up 'creed' he found on the internet and he wants Dr. Sylvan to apply it somehow to the case at hand. That's improper."

Quinn looked back at Brunelle. "Response?"

Brunelle had been ready for the objection. "Mr. Jacobsen started down this road when he had Dr. Sylvan give his opinion that Ms. Belfair's death wasn't manslaughter. I should now be allowed to explore the basis for that opinion and challenge it."

Quinn closed her eyes for a moment. The case was on the edge of descending into the X-rated explicitness she had vowed to avoid.

"I won't get into details, Your Honor," Brunelle offered. "If the witness could simply read the exhibit to himself, that should be sufficient for me to complete my examination."

Quinn opened her eyes again, and her mouth twisted into a tight knot. But, after a moment, she ruled, "Objection overruled."

Jacobsen nodded and sat down. Brunelle moved in for, what he hoped would be, the kill.

"Are you familiar with the creed printed on that document?"

Sylvan tried to shrug it off. "I've seen several similar writings. I'm not sure if I've ever read this particular version. Probably."

"The basic point is that in this sort of uncommon relationship, the role of the Master isn't just about being dominant during sex, correct?"

Sylvan thought for a moment. "I think that's a fair summary. They tend to emphasize the responsibilities of the dominant to his submissive."

"Because it's not just about sex, right? It's about the entire relationship."

Sylvan obviously liked that. "Correct," he agreed quickly.

Brunelle followed up almost as quickly. A series of questions delivered just quickly enough to encourage Sylvan's agreement, but just slowly enough to make sure the jury could follow along.

"The submissive loves her master, correct?"

"Correct."

"And the submissive trusts her master, correct?"

"That's also correct."

"And the submissive gives up her body to the protection and control of her master, correct?"

"Yes. That's correct."

Then the reverse. The corollary. The whole point.

"The master also loves his submissive, correct?" Brunelle continued.

"Correct."

"And the master willingly accepts his submissive's trust, correct?"

"Correct."

"And in so doing, the master accepts the responsibility of protecting his submissive, correct?"

Sylvan paused. But he couldn't deny it. "Yes, that's correct."

Brunelle finally paused, but only for dramatic effect. To make sure the jury was caught up, and paying attention. Then he delivered the pay-off question:

"Mr. Atkins failed that responsibility, didn't he, Dr. Sylvan? He betrayed her trust. He failed to protect her. Isn't that right?"

Sylvan thought for a moment. Then another. Then longer still. Too long. Everyone knew the answer he had to finally admit. "Yes, I suppose he did."

"A reasonable master should have known Tina was at risk and should have protected her, correct?"

Sylvan paused again, but he wasn't going to lie. "Yes. I suppose that's correct."

So," Brunelle summed up. "Judging Mr. Atkins within the context, and with a full understanding of, his special relationship with Ms. Belfair, he didn't act like a reasonable master, did he?"

"No."

"He was a reckless master, wasn't he?"

Sylvan paused as long as he could. Then admitted, "Yes. He was reckless."

No pause at all from Brunelle. "Tina Belfair died as a result of that recklessness, didn't she?"

Sylvan frowned ever so slightly. "I suppose she did."

Brunelle smiled ever so slightly. "No further questions."

CHAPTER 41

"How do you plead," Judge Quinn asked Master Michael while the jury waited, ignorantly, in the jury room, "to the reduced charge of manslaughter in the second degree?"

Mid-trial plea bargains weren't the norm, but they weren't uncommon either. Every witness, every question and answer, changed the odds of prevailing for one side or the other. Sometimes, overconfident defendants saw the writing on the wall. Sometimes, overconfident prosecutors realized that the defendant probably didn't see the risk and disregard it--he just should have seen the risk and didn't. That was Manslaughter 2.

Atkins looked to his attorney for confirmation and Jacobsen nodded. Atkins sighed and looked up at the judge. "Guilty."

Quinn nodded. Brunelle exhaled. Atkins steeled himself for the sentence.

He had no criminal history, so he would get the lowest possible sentence. If he'd been convicted of Man 1, he was looking at seven to nine years. On Man 2, he'd only get 22 months. With good time, he'd only serve fifteen of those. He'd start at a minimum security prison, but after nine months, he'd be transferred to a work release facility. Six months later he'd be out on the streets again. It wouldn't be the best fifteen months of his life, but it beat the risk of nine years on the inside. Especially after his own expert told the jury he was responsible for Tina's death.

Quinn imposed the 22 months, and Atkins was remanded into custody. That was the time the judge usually let the defendant say goodbye to his family before disappearing into the secured hallways that led to the jail. But Atkins didn't have any family to say goodbye to. He'd killed her.

No one else came to the watch the plea. Except Robyn. She sat silently in the back, looking through files as if she were working on her cases and only minimally aware of the proceedings. After Atkins was taken away, Jacobsen began packing up his things. Once the attorneys were also gone, the judge would bring the jurors out from the jury room where they'd been waiting and wondering what was going on, and explain to them that their services were no longer required. Brunelle supposed there was nothing more frustrating to a juror than to sit through almost an entire trial only to have the decision ripped away by the damned lawyers.

Brunelle didn't wait to shake Jacobsen's hand. The defense attorney wasn't looking his way anyway, and, more importantly, Robyn stood up and headed out into the hallway. Brunelle decided to skip the niceties with his opposing counsel and follow his lover out of the courtroom.

She was waiting for him.

"Well done, Mr. B," she said with a light smile. "That's a good result."

Brunelle smiled back. "For him or me? I would have preferred the Man One, but then again, I guess he would have preferred an acquittal. They say the best plea bargains are the ones when no one is happy."

Robyn smiled and nodded. "Yeah, I've heard that too. That's bullshit."

Brunelle was taken aback by her abruptness.

"The best plea bargains," she declared, "are the ones that are just."

Brunelle's smile returned. He nodded. "I guess that's true."

Robyn cocked her head. "So, was that a just result?"

Brunelle thought for a moment. He nodded again. "I think so. It would have been hard to prove he knew Tina might die and didn't care. It's more like he should have known there was a danger and he was too stupid that night to realize it. That's probably what happened, so that was probably a just result."

Robyn stepped up to him. "I agree." She kissed him on the cheek. "It's hot that you seek justice."

Brunelle's heart raced. He sought more than that. He grabbed her by the waist and pulled her against him, kissing her fully on the mouth. She didn't resist, even in the courthouse hallway. But after a moment, she pulled away. Without another word, she tapped her finger on her nose and walked away.

Brunelle watched her retreating form, remembering his views of her backside from the previous night. His heart, and other body parts, were swelling, so it was doubly shocking when he turned back to see Kat staring at him from the other end of the hallway.

"Uh," he started. "That's not what it looked like."

Of course they both knew it was exactly what it looked like.

"Larry called and told me you got your defendant to plead out," Kat explained, her voice trembling at the edges. "I came down to congratulate you and see if you wanted to grab lunch."

"Lunch?" he repeated. As if that's what they were talking about any more.

"I guess," Kat went on, "now I know why you've been so distant."

Brunelle wasn't sure what to say. So he didn't say anything.

"I—" She was holding back the tears, but her fists were clenched and shaking. "I thought we—" But she couldn't finish.

"Look, Kat," Brunelle started. "It's complicated."

At that Kat laughed darkly. Her voice found its footing. The edges were hard again. "No, it's not complicated. It's simple. Good bye, David."

She too turned and walked away. Brunelle again watched the retreating form and couldn't help but remember better times.

Jacobsen came out of the courtroom then. Maybe Brunelle should have said something. Congratulated him on a well fought trial, or something like that. But Brunelle ignored him and started back toward his office, his heart heavy and conscience upended.

He couldn't have cared less about that stupid fucking case.

EPILOGUE

Michael Atkins was in prison. Ron Jacobsen was on to his next case. Yvonne Taylor closed her investigation with a sternly worded warning letter. Kat Anderson didn't return Brunelle's one voicemail. And Larry Chen was deeply disappointed in his friend the D.A.

And Robyn Dunn was still full of surprises.

Brunelle hadn't seen her for a few days. She'd also failed to return any of his texts or voicemails, of which there were many. He finally ran into her outside of the Pit one afternoon—after running her bar number and seeing what hearing she had that day. He didn't try to kiss her again, not in the courthouse hallway, but he let his intentions be known.

"So do you want to grab dinner or something?" he asked, a bit lamely. He knew it.

She did too. "You mean," she translated, "do I want to get together and fuck, and maybe we eat something beforehand?"

Brunelle smiled self-consciously, but he didn't correct her.

So she corrected him.

"Look, Dave. I think you're a really nice guy. You're a good lawyer and for a prosecutor, you're not a complete ass."

Brunelle's heart knew exactly where this was headed, but his brain latched on to the words to avoid acknowledging their purpose.

"Uh, thanks. I guess."

"But you're still a prosecutor," she went on. Her slight smile fading. The dimple disappeared. "And I'm still a defense attorney. It's fine that we hooked up a couple of times, but we can't make this work. Not long term."

Brunelle started to argue but Robyn cut him off.

"It was fun," she said. "But it's over."

Brunelle admired her honesty. And her candor. And he managed not to cry as she walked away.

END

THE DAVID BRUNELLE LEGAL THRILLERS
Presumption of Innocence
Tribal Court
By Reason of Insanity
A Prosecutor for the Defense
Substantial Risk
Corpus Delicti
Accomplice Liability
A Lack of Motive
Missing Witness
Diminished Capacity
Devil's Plea Bargain
Homicide in Berlin
Premeditated Intent
Alibi Defense
Defense of Others

THE TALON WINTER LEGAL THRILLERS
Winter's Law
Winter's Chance
Winter's Reason
Winter's Justice
Winter's Duty
Winter's Passion

ALSO BY STEPHEN PENNER
Scottish Rite
Blood Rite
Last Rite
Mars Station Alpha
The Godling Club

ABOUT THE AUTHOR

Stephen Penner is an attorney, author, and artist from Seattle.

In addition to writing the *David Brunelle Legal Thriller Series*, he is also the author of the *Talon Winter Legal Thrillers*, starring Tacoma criminal defense attorney Talon Winter; the *Maggie Devereaux Paranormal Mysteries*, recounting the exploits of an American graduate student in the magical Highlands of Scotland; and several stand-alone works.

For more information, please visit *www.stephenpenner.com*.